Also by Frances McNamara

ෆ

Death at Hull House
An Emily Cabot Mystery

DEATH
AT
THE FAIR

Frances McNamara

 ALLIUM PRESS OF CHICAGO

Allium Press of Chicago
www.alliumpress.com

This is a work of fiction. Descriptions and portrayals
of real people, events, organizations, or
establishments are intended to provide background
for the story and are used fictitiously. Other
characters and situations are drawn from the author's
imagination and are not intended to be real.

Revised edition by Allium Press, 2009
Originally published via BookSurge, 2008

Book and cover design by E. C. Victorson

Front cover image (bottom) from *The World's Fair in Water Colors*
by Charles S. Graham, 1893

ISBN-13: 978-0-9840676-1-9

For my parents

Marie and Ed McNamara

Death at the Fair

&

ONE

The Fair was a great undertaking. Forgotten now, I am amazed to remember how quickly traces of it were dispersed, carted away, burnt to the ground or overgrown by plants in the park that remained. By the end, only the Palace of Fine Arts stood, as if struggling to maintain some vestige of a ruined civilization, providing only an echo of what had been. The lone relic, it finally became the Museum of Science and Industry in one of those many transformations that we have experienced in the twentieth century.

Despite that so rapid disappearance, like some fairy city that had existence only at twilight, I find when I remember it now, the White City of the World's Columbian Exposition exists in my mind whole and complete as it looked in the early summer days of 1893 when you could still look down on the Court of Honor from the roof of the Manufactures and Liberal Arts Building. The graceful white structures with their long colonnades and statues surrounded a basin of water where gondolas floated peacefully. At one end, the great Columbian Fountain with its flowing figures celebrated the deeds of its namesake as they paddled a fantastic ark.

That summer we felt we were at the heart of the universe as people from all over the world traveled to Chicago to visit the Fair. And I think we were all proud and a little overwhelmed by the scope of human accomplishments represented in the huge buildings, which contained exhibits of everything from electricity, machinery and mines to agriculture and the fine arts. But, in the end, it was the events that overtook me in the final days of the Fair that came to tinge the memory of that display with a kind of wistful melancholy. It was as if the potential greatness was so near to our grasp but at the last minute slipped away, like a match sheltered in cupped hands that goes out in a draft.

I remained in Chicago over the summer to recover from an illness and to complete the research I began in my first year of graduate study at the University of Chicago. That work required the tedious compilation of statistics from thousands of identity cards provided by the Chicago Police Department. The result was something less than it might have been without the loss of some of the cards and of the original draft, which happened during my illness, but my professor, Mr. Reed, was well satisfied. And perhaps more importantly, I was confident that it was a piece of research good enough to bolster Dean Talbot's arguments that the fellowship support for my work should continue, although only six of these honors had been granted to women. While all the world had come to visit the great Exposition at our doorstep, I had been bent over my desk taking time only to tend to the duties that paid for my room and board.

By late August my work was done and I was free to explore the Fair as I had not been able to do earlier. My mother and brother traveled from Boston and I found them rooms in university dormitories that had been appropriated for the use of Fair visitors. Only that made the trip affordable for them. I was myself still employed in managing the women's housing and spent mornings at the desk in one of the alcoves of the Manufactures and Liberal Arts Building where I assisted members of the Women's Collegiate Association in booking rooms.

It was on one such day that I completed my shift and threaded my way, through the crowds viewing the magnificent wrought iron gateways of the German exhibit, to the southwestern portico, where I had left my mother sitting on a bench.

The day was hot, but inside the high ceilings and vast spaces retained a coolness. Outside, the portico provided shade and a slight zephyr of breeze that gave some relief. My mother was a tiny figure in her black widow's weeds. It was five years now since my father's tragic and unexpected death, yet she had never felt the need to leave her mourning clothes behind. It was not that she was unable to resign herself to her situation or that she was unduly morose about his absence, but I think she felt the lack of his presence beside her everyday. I had given up trying to encourage her to change her wardrobe. She just felt no need to do that.

"Mother, here I am. But where is Alden? Surely he should have been here by now?"

My younger brother was demonstrating his usual fecklessness. Never an ardent student, at nineteen he had discontinued his studies at Harvard and taken a job at our uncle's bank. He had been given time off to accompany my mother on this trip only by virtue of her wealthy brother's favor. This day, he was supposed to have escorted my mother to meet me but she had arrived alone saying he had stopped somewhere on the Midway and would be along shortly. Her tolerance for his undependable nature always exasperated me.

"I'm sure he will be here soon, Emily. You mustn't worry. Is this perhaps the doctor coming now?" She nodded and I turned around to see Dr. Stephen Chapman coming up the steps. Hatless, he mounted without haste, looking around him as if to take in the expanse of buildings and people. With a clean-shaven square face, warm brown eyes and dark hair always in need of a trim, the doctor seemed old to me at that time, although he was only in his mid-thirties. A physician who had given up his practice to do research at the new university, he had quickly gained a reputation for brilliance in his laboratory studies. He had been quite helpful in the early days when construction delays had us all scrambling to make do in temporary quarters at the Hotel Beatrice. Unlike most of the impatient male professors he had been grateful for the household tasks we women took on to compensate at the beginning. Once we were all settled into our real housing and studies, my friend Clara and I had put out some efforts to try to pry the doctor from his microscope to join us at social functions. Today I saw he wore the same brown suit that had sufficed for all the classes and university functions during the preceding year. The thought of that wool made me feel itchy on such a sultry day but he was the same as always, quiet, thoughtful and just a little aloof. Reaching the top step, he made a slight bow to my mother as I introduced him and she held out her hand.

"Dear Dr. Chapman, we are greatly in your debt. I cannot tell you how grateful I am to you for saving my daughter. She told me you would not wish to be thanked but you would not blame me if you knew how often I have shuddered to imagine what might have happened if you had not been there."

I felt the blood rise to the tips of my ears. I had fallen ill of a fever during the spring quarter but I thought my mother exaggerated my danger. At the time, I had been much more concerned that the weakness would prevent me from continuing at the university than that it would be mortal.

"I am grateful to have been able to spare you such pain. Luckily, Miss Cabot has a healthy constitution and her recovery has been complete, so you have nothing to worry about."

"Yes, Mother, I am completely recovered. Please don't doubt that. It was only with the help of Dr. Chapman that I was allowed to extend my course work through the summer to complete it. At one point Professor Lukas and some of the others were insisting that my illness proved women could not sustain the rigors of advanced work. I very nearly lost my fellowship."

"Dean Talbot would not have allowed that," he told my mother. "She and Dean Palmer are themselves the strongest evidence that such carping is unjustified."

"The dean told me how Dr. Chapman put down the critics, Mother. He embarrassed them by recounting their own past illnesses as evidence that male scholars are every bit as apt to suffer as the women. He was our champion."

"Foolishness. I merely told them the truth. But, in any case, Mrs. Cabot, your daughter is fully recovered. We all of us have to suffer from sickness at one time or another. In some ways it can be said to strengthen us. There are certainly cases where having once experienced an illness we are afterwards protected from it."

It was kind of him to reassure her and we spent some minutes discussing my mother's journey from Boston. My illness had resulted in a sudden intimacy with the doctor and when I was fully recovered and busy with the task of completing my research I soon found I missed his daily visits. I had come to know him only a very little during that time. He never spoke of family and seemed quite alone in the world. Despite the fact that he, too, had remained at the university to pursue his studies over the summer, I was seldom able to lure him from the beakers and microscopes of his laboratory. But I was determined he would not miss a tour of the great sights of the Fair for lack of company.

Yet, it was only by appealing to his kindness and pity for my widowed mother that I had finally persuaded him to join us on our expeditions during her visit. He seemed at once grateful and somewhat reluctant to be included in our party yet I knew him to be an intelligent man who could not help but be stimulated by the great variety of ideas and novelties we would find in the exhibits. The truth was that I hoped my mother's warmth would draw him out and I was looking forward to days spent touring the Fair followed by lively discussions of what we had seen over dinners and suppers. I felt I had earned the respite after a tedious summer, and so had the doctor. Now I looked around, exasperated by my brother's failure to arrive on time. It was so like him.

"I'm sorry my brother is late. I told him we would meet here at one o'clock to begin our tour. I can't imagine what is keeping him."

"I'm afraid my son, Alden, is easily distracted by the amusements of the Midway, Dr. Chapman. He stopped there on our way over but I am sure he will join us shortly, and if he does not, we can begin without him."

"With all the wonders of art and industry to be seen, my brother thinks only of amusements. It is a shame," I complained. I was vexed. It had been difficult enough to persuade the doctor to join us and now Alden was making us wait.

"Quite a few people are finding the exhibits on the Midway every bit as attractive as the more formal exhibitions," he said dryly. "They say it is far more profitable than the Fair itself."

"Emily, I believe someone is trying to get your attention," my mother gestured towards the sunlight.

The shaded portico overlooked the promenade along the Basin. As I turned, I saw a group of elegant women with parasols strolling towards us.

"Clara!" I raced down the steps and we embraced.

I had missed Clara Shea ever since she returned home to Kentucky in June, and I had not expected to see her again until the fall quarter began. Like me, she came to the university when it opened the previous fall as one of the first women graduate students and we became good friends and allies. Today Clara made a striking figure with her piles of dark hair pinned up under a straw boater. She looked magnificent in a summer frock of frothy white with black dots and black velvet trim. I knew I must appear dowdy beside my tall friend in my shirtwaist and brown skirt but I had become used to her impressive beauty and I was delighted to see her when I had never expected it. I immediately knew that her company would make the excursions to the Fair perfect from my point of view.

"My gram finally decided we should come to view the Fair after all," she confided in a low voice and her breathy Southern drawl. "I do believe she got tired of having to listen to everyone else tell her stories about their trips." She turned back to the others who were slowly coming up behind her. "Gram, here is Emily Cabot. I told you all about her."

She was a small woman with bright eyes who wore an elegant suit of lavender and held a silver walking stick. Clara frequently quoted her grandmother and I was curious to meet this woman who had been so important in her support for her granddaughter's education. From what my friend had told me, it was her grandmother who had responded to Clara's broken engagement by handing her a prospectus for the new university and it was she who had insisted on the feasibility of the plan despite the objections of other family members. It seemed a great deal of warm charm sheathed an adamant resolution of will in this small woman. So different physically, I suspected she and Clara were very similar underneath.

Beyond her two more women in the party appeared to waft rather than walk. They wore pastel dresses with matching parasols. One was middle-aged and by her resemblance to Clara, as if she were a slightly more attenuated and delicate version, I guessed she must be my friend's mother.

The other woman was younger, although not as young as Clara and myself, displaying none of the awkwardness of youth but rather a languid elegance. She had an abstracted, faraway look in her blue eyes and only wisps of pale hair escaped along her cheekbones under a hat adorned with ostrich feathers. A web of white lace touched her throat and wrists. I sensed an air of sadness that was like a fine mist hanging around her.

Remembering my own companions, I turned back and saw my mother descending the small flight of steps on Dr. Chapman's arm. I caught him looking up from his care of guiding her to glance at the newcomers, and I thought I saw a sign of recognition. But the next moment he was attending to my mother's progress again and I thought it must have been my imagination.

Clara handled the round of introductions. The woman who so resembled her was indeed her mother and the other woman was introduced as Mrs. Larrimer, another Kentuckian come to view the Fair with her husband and father. As I turned to look at her again I saw that the woman's blue eyes were fixed on Dr. Chapman's face. She did not respond to Clara's words and her air of elegance had suddenly deserted her. I was close enough to hear her whisper his name, "Stephen."

Dr. Chapman acknowledged the acquaintance reluctantly, I thought. "I was a student of Mrs. Larrimer's father," he told the rest of us. Then turning back to her, "I trust he is in good health?"

She tore her eyes from his face and bowed her head. "He has traveled with us to attend the medical congress here. He would be happy to see you again." She had a low voice and spoke slowly. He bowed.

"I am sure we will meet in that case, as I also attend the congress."

"Her father and her husband were too busy attending to their own affairs to accompany Marguerite today, Doctor," Clara's grandmother told him. "But we are not ones to wait on the gentlemen, so we carried her off with us to see the sights." She leaned on her cane and looked around at the bustling fair grounds. "Although, I must say, I am quite liable to be overwhelmed by the number and size of these buildings. I think we must consult on how best to start on them, ladies, as we will not be allowed to miss any seriously important thing. Not with two such ardent scholars to guide us."

"Don't worry, Gram," Clara told her. "I have the map and I see that Emily brought a guidebook. Together we will guarantee you will not escape a single truly important exhibit. I'd thought to see the Woman's Building—I know it will interest Gram, don't you think, Emily?"

As I held out the guidebook to her I could see, from the corner of my eye, that Mrs. Larrimer had once again lifted her eyes and was staring at Dr. Chapman.

"You have come from Baltimore?" she asked him softly.

He grimaced. "I reside here in Chicago. I have been here since last year studying at the university."

"You gave up your practice then?"

He nodded curtly and shifted as if the wool suit, that looked so scratchy to me, was finally wearing on him. They were on the edge of our group and had spoken softly, almost as if continuing a conversation from some time in the past, while Clara and her mother argued about our proposed route. Somehow I was curious enough to be straining to hear them. Suddenly the doctor interrupted Clara.

"And now, if you ladies will excuse me, I must return to my laboratory."

"But, Dr. Chapman, I thought you would join us for the tour," I told him. His eyes shifted to mine and I thought a slight bit of color tinged his cheeks.

"You must excuse me, Miss Cabot. I did not have a chance to explain my change of plans. There is an experiment I must attend to in the laboratory. I came myself, so that I might at least meet your mother and brother, but I cannot stay. Please accept my apologies. I am sure you have found much better companions for your tour."

He bade us farewell with a slight bow and began to stride away. As the others returned to their discussion I hurried after him, calling, "Doctor!" He could not fail to hear me so he had to respond. He stopped. His neck was red as he turned back to me.

"You will join us for supper later, won't you?" We had planned to go to a hotel in Hyde Park.

He glanced back over my head. "Please, convey my apologies to your mother and brother," he said. "I will be unable to join you."

"But, Dr. Chapman, what is it? Is something wrong? I hope we have not offended you? I wanted so much for you to join us. My mother has wanted to meet you and you will enjoy my brother even if he is unreliable and I thought we would have such an interesting and instructive time, discussing what we had seen. All together."

"Oh, I think you will have plenty of company with Miss Shea and her party." He was looking over my shoulder.

"But so much of the world is on display here, Doctor. Surely you don't want to miss it? You told me you wanted to visit the Fine Arts Building. And you said you had heard much about the German exhibit in the Manufactures Building. You can spare the time for that, can't you? We can be sure to put those first on the tour and you could join us later at the hotel . . ."

"No, I cannot. I am sorry." He pulled his gaze away from the group behind me to look me in the eye. "Your friends are waiting. By all means begin your tour. You do not need me. Now, I must return to my laboratory."

When he turned away that time I had no choice but to let him go. He would not be moved. Trying to persuade him when he had made up his mind was like stubbing your toe on what seemed to be a loose pebble and was really a substantial rock embedded in the ground.

I couldn't help frowning as I looked back at the elegant Mrs. Larrimer whose eyes were following the figure of Dr. Chapman as he disappeared into the crowd. Who was this woman and what was she to my friend? I was sure that it had been the unexpected meeting that caused him to return to his research, thereby ruining all my plans. Naively I assumed their past association must have ended in some disagreement or unpleasantness. I shook myself. The sun shone brightly as hundreds of figures strolled through the wide boulevards lined by the massive buildings of the White City. Whatever was bothering the two of them it was no business of mine and no reason for me to waste an afternoon that was meant to be spent viewing the many new and important things on display at the exposition. Only it irked me that both the doctor and Alden had managed to foil my plan. At least Clara's arrival was an improvement.

TWO

*D*isappointed, I returned to the group of women to find that Clara and her mother were arguing about where to go first. Clara's grandmother turned to me, placing her walking stick in front of her and leaning on it with both hands.

"So, this is Emily. And that was Dr. Chapman who brought you back from the brink of death from what Clara told me. Pay no mind, my dear. No doubt the doctor is overwhelmed by too many women. It is a brave man who can face being so outnumbered. We will not let his desertion sway us. But surely there must be some place where we can all sit down and take some refreshments before we visit any of these magnificent and quite lengthy exhibits."

We consulted and decided to stop at the Marine Café before touring the Electricity Building. Clara and I were the ones most interested in the arrangements. My mother looked on happily, enjoying our enthusiasm, while Clara's mother occasionally criticized our plan when she thought we proposed too strenuous a schedule, and Mrs. Larrimer did not take part in the discussion at all. That lady stood staring dreamily out at the gondolas as they floated past on the Basin. We were about to make our way to the café when my brother finally rushed up, straw boater in hand.

"Alden, where have you been?" I snapped.

He grinned and twirled the hat in his hands. "Sorry. I had to see a man."

I glared at him while my mother made the introductions. Five years my junior, my only brother appeared even younger. He was slight of build, and inherited a mop of dark curls from our father, but his bright blue eyes were from our mother's side of the family. I, on the other hand, have only our father's brown eyes and the wispy lighter hair of our mother. Alden was quick on his feet, not only physically graceful but fearless in activities like climbing trees or riding horses. When we were growing up he could always beat me at any game that required the mind, yet his undisciplined ways made him unsuccessful in his studies, much to our father's dismay. But he had an easy manner and a curious temperament that charmed men and women alike. My younger sister, Rose, who was now a married woman in society, wrote that he had gained the affections of several eligible young women but she despaired of his ever making a match due to his fickleness. In the family preoccupation with what to do about Alden, Rose clearly thought he should marry some wealthy young lady but I knew he was too quick to ever be caught in that trap.

"You must ride the Ferris Wheel," he told us as Clara and I led the way to the café, consulting our maps. My brother was the sort of person who never consulted a map and always found his way by instinct.

"Alden, have you been spending your money already on such trifles? You're supposed to be here to view the educational exhibits and to escort Mama, not to run off to the Midway every chance you get."

"My sister is so serious, Miss Shea. She hardly ever gets her nose out of a book."

I stopped to consult my guidebook again but he grabbed it from my hand and leapt up onto the stone balustrade that lined the Basin. "Alden, be careful."

Clara was laughing.

I cringed as he stood on tiptoe and compared his view to the page.

"And she would walk our poor mother and your grandmother off their feet if I didn't interfere." He jumped back to the ground. "There," he said, pointing.

He went striding through the crowd and when we followed, sure enough, he had found the café. He reached the shaded pavilion of tables ahead of us and was talking to a waiter who waved us to a table when we caught up. "You see what happens when you look beyond your book," he said as he handed it back to me. He was very self satisfied. I ignored him and settled myself beside Clara.

We ordered tea and sandwiches and made our plans sitting on the iron furniture of a porch overlooking Lake Michigan. My mother and Clara's grandmother appeared to make friends easily while Alden took it upon himself to amuse Mrs. Shea and Mrs. Larrimer with his chatter.

"What a shame Dr. Chapman couldn't join us, Emily." Clara and I had decided the route and were finishing the last of the sandwiches.

"I thought I had persuaded him," I confessed. "He has been working in the laboratory all summer, so he has not even seen the exhibits. He confessed it to me. I don't know how he can ignore such a magnificent display as the Fair, right here in Hyde Park. But I suppose he must do as he pleases." I shrugged. "But who is this Mrs. Larrimer, Clara? And how does she know the doctor? I think it was meeting her unexpectedly that sent him scurrying back to his microscope."

Clara was gazing across at Mrs. Larrimer who listened to Alden with a slight smile on her face. "Mrs. Larrimer is married to a wealthy cotton dealer. His family had a plantation before the war but his father and brothers all died. He was the only one left and he rebuilt the family fortunes by trading in cotton. They say he adores his wife but there is some tragedy that happened in the past. I never have heard the whole story. My mother just shakes her head and says, 'poor Marguerite.' I wonder what happened." We both looked at the beautiful woman whose gloved fingers played with her parasol. Clara turned to me.

"But you should meet her husband, he is a very impressive man. I am not sure what to think of him, Emily, I know. There is a concert and supper at the Music Hall tomorrow night after the medical congress. You must come. I'm sure that Dr. Chapman will not miss it. You know how he loves music." It was true. We had discovered that music was one of the few things that could entice the doctor from his research.

"I think you need an invitation for those events."

"Oh, but I'm sure we can get you one. Gram," she turned to her grandmother. "Wouldn't it be wonderful if Emily and her mother and Alden could join us tomorrow night for the festivities?"

My mother and I demurred since we were not attending the conference, and the concert was planned for participants. But Alden caught the drift of the conversation and eagerly agreed. The elder Mrs. Shea told us that Mrs. Larrimer's father was one of the primary organizers and assured us we would receive an invitation.

With that settled, we were ready to begin the strenuous tour that Clara and I had devised. We spent the rest of the afternoon walking through several of the immense buildings. Electricity was especially dramatic with the dark tomb of an Egyptian Temple illuminated by electric light and there was a Kinetoscope machine that ran moving pictures. Alden insisted on standing in line to view that a second time while the rest of us went on. People were making telephone calls to Boston at one exhibit, which fascinated my mother, and we were all impressed by the tower of light at the center.

In Mines we walked down Bullion Boulevard and saw displays of metals and jewels, and a solid silver statue of a New York actress. In Machinery, Alden found a place where we could ride a platform that was lifted by a crane which had been used to build the structure and was now located inside of it.

We broke into parties as we toured so that my mother and the elder Mrs. Shea could frequently find a bench on which to rest, while Clara and I paid great attention to the exhibits, and the two married ladies drifted slowly. Alden flitted around from group to group and shepherded us back together when he judged we had spent sufficient time in one building and ought to move on despite my protests.

Back in the Manufactures Building we found my mother and Clara's grandmother viewing a certain display with doubtful expressions. It was for a wheat manufacturer and the exhibit was in the form of a huge barrel. In front of it, a Negro woman of substantial proportions wearing a kerchief in her hair was cooking pancakes. She was known as Aunt Jemima and she entertained the crowds by telling colorful stories of plantation life in the South.

My parents had been abolitionists before the war and my mother questioned the taste of this display. Clara's grandmother, on the other hand, had grown up on a plantation and she questioned the accuracy of the stories. Alden, of course, managed to get a plate of the pancakes and offered it around to the group for a taste. While we stood there commenting on the flavors, I noticed a slightly strange scene that I was to remember later.

Mrs. Larrimer had refused a taste of the pancakes and drifted away from us towards the next exhibit. I remember hearing Clara's grandmother comment, "Marguerite is a Northern woman transplanted to one of our Southern plantations. I am afraid she will never feel quite at home there." But no one paid any attention to the straggler. Now, I saw that the elegant blonde lady was being approached by a young Negro man. She came to a sudden halt when she saw him.

He was a well-dressed young man in a suit who stepped away from a group of other Negroes. They had just noticed Aunt Jemima and were moving towards the large barrel. Leaving him behind, unnoticed, they proceeded forwards while he came to a stop, staring at Mrs. Larrimer. A look of surprise crossed his face to be replaced by a look of anxiety. He bowed politely but she was already backing away from him, keeping her furled parasol between them. He raised his hands as if pleading and I was about to comment on the scene when she pirouetted around, her skirts swirling, and marched back to us. The young man just stood there watching, then bowed his head. It was all over quickly and he made no move to follow her, so I let my attention return to the comments of my group. I glanced at Mrs. Larrimer when she rejoined us, but she had nothing to say about the encounter, so I thought it would be rude to mention it. I joined the general discussion of what to do next instead.

We decided we had accomplished enough for our first day and as Alden led us unerringly to the Midway exit where our friends would meet their carriage, we said our good-byes.

"We'll see you tomorrow night, then." Clara hugged me. I was less sure of that but knew we could reach them at the Palmer House where her grandmother had a suite of rooms.

After dinner at a hotel, we finally reached our own rooms. By that time, my mother and I were glad to sit quietly.

"I'm sorry Dr. Chapman was unable to join us," she commented as we prepared to retire for the night.

I shook my head. I was embarrassed that I had been mistaken in my assumptions that the doctor would be spending time with us during her visit. I felt very foolish. "I thought he had agreed to do so but he must have had work to attend to. He is very devoted to his studies."

My mother looked at me from the corner of her eye as she folded a shawl. "I thought perhaps meeting Mrs. Larrimer so unexpectedly discomposed him. He murmured her name, 'Marguerite', as he helped me down the stairs. Were they well acquainted in the past?"

"I have no idea." It annoyed me that I knew so little about his past. "He studied at Johns Hopkins in Baltimore. I have never seen her before, nor has he ever mentioned her or her father. He was in practice at one time, I know, perhaps that is how he knew them. But he gave that up to continue his studies."

She finished her task without speaking and the silence made me uneasy.

"It is too bad that Father is not around to keep Alden in hand," I said impulsively. I never meant to pain her with the memory of my father's loss but sometimes I sorely missed his influence.

She sighed. "You must not be too hard on Alden, Emily." She stood up straight and looked me in the eye. "When your father was alive they quarreled frequently. Alden feels it very deeply that he never lived up to your father's expectations. But that is how it is sometimes between fathers and sons, Emily. And it is something your brother greatly regrets, although he may often fail to show it. Alden will never be like your father. Of the children, you are most like him, you know. And he would have been very proud to see you now, continuing your studies."

She patted my hand and I felt badly for what I had said. I knew I could say no more about it although I longed to have someone to talk to, so I went to sleep, hoping fervently that I would see Clara again soon.

In the morning, sure enough, we received a gilt edged invitation to the concert and supper at the Music Hall.

THREE

*T*he next afternoon there was a note from Dr. Chapman asking if he could escort us to the concert. Clara had invited him to be one of the party, shrewdly realizing that the doctor would not turn down a chance to hear the orchestra as he had a great love of music. But I was greatly surprised and considered it a fine compliment that he offered to take us—me, in particular. It certainly made up for my embarrassment the day before and I was grateful to him for it.

We returned early from the Fair that day in order to rest and prepare for the evening and were ready when the doctor called for us. Our walk through the mild night took us the length of the Basin in the Court of Honor, my mother and I walking arm and arm behind the two men as Alden engaged the doctor in a dispute over the relative merits of Russian composers. We wondered at the great illuminations of electric light that turned the collection of buildings into a dramatic display doubled by the reflections in the water.

The Music Hall was at the northeast corner of the Basin and was in the classical style of all those buildings with Corinthian columns and statues, standing up against the fading light of the sky. A crowd of people in evening clothes made their way into the barrel-vaulted hall decorated with paintings of leaves and gold trim on the woodwork. They came to hear the orchestra play *Scheherazade* by Rimsky-Korsakov, evoking an alien world of incense and silk. As I walked down the promenade of the White

19

City—as the Fair was known, for its uniformly ivory facades—and joined a company dressed in rich silks and jewels, I could almost believe I existed in some foreign world far from the dirty workaday city or the gray stone of the university. I was almost sorry when the music ended but I was glad to find Clara in the crowd and to be led by her to the large supper table in an alcove that had been reserved for our party.

To my surprise I found myself seated at the right hand of Mr. Charles Larrimer, who was our host, with Dr. Chapman, my mother, and Alden ordered beside me. Opposite sat a Mr. Fitzgibbons, Mrs. Larrimer, and her father, Dr. Ramsey. Clara and her relatives were at the other end. Alden had managed to seat himself near them and away from the danger of serious conversation. But I was happy to find myself near our host. Since coming to the university I felt I had a place in the world of more importance than I had ever had before. I was proud of the kind of research I was involved in and I appreciated the respect it inspired in others. Mr. Charles Larrimer was holding court from the head of the table and I felt myself willing and able to participate.

He was an impressively handsome man. Tall and thin, he wore an elegant set of evening clothes that clung to him perfectly, the onyx studs and miniscule embroidery of the white shirt providing a quiet assurance of the care and expense of his clothing. His handsome face appeared unlined although he must have been in his forties, some twenty years older than me, and some ten years his wife's senior. He had fine golden hair with neatly clipped sideburns and moustache. His movements reminded me of Alden in their grace and fluidity but I had the impression he would never be so heedless as my brother tended to be. On the contrary, each movement was executed with a slow rhythm like the list of his Southern accent, which seemed to slow all of his speeches to a leisured cadence. But it was the blue eyes that were his most apparent feature. They appeared mild and glassy as a pond reflecting a tranquil sky most times but later they would become quite startlingly sharp and icy in a way that was very unexpected.

The man opposite me could not be more different. Introduced as Mr. Peter Francis Fitzgibbons, but generally referred to as Fitz, he was a representative of Chicago's mayor, Carter Harrison. His duties at the moment appeared to consist of squiring around the wealthy Southerner and greasing his way whenever needed. He must have been about the same age as Mr. Larrimer but his face was weathered and rough where not hidden by huge muttonchop sideburns and a large moustache. Where every stitch in the other man's elegant evening clothes appeared to have been sewn to conform to his body, Mr. Fitzgibbons's impeccable and probably expensive version seemed a little too small for his large frame. When you looked at him you knew immediately that he belonged in a bowler hat with woolen coat and vest, even in summer. His genial hazel eyes assessed the group from under hairy eyebrows with just a few gray strands and there was almost always a smile on his face.

His proportions made Mrs. Larrimer appear even more delicate as she sat, tall and straight-backed, beside him. She wore a diaphanous ivory gown threaded with silver in the shape of falling leaves and around her throat was a choker of four strands of pearls with more magnificent long strands falling in large loops to her waist. Her father, Dr. Ramsey, sat even taller and straighter beside her with a high domed forehead and full beard carefully trimmed over an impeccable suit of evening clothes.

I remember feeling distinctly impressed by such distinguished company as I was so politely invited to take my seat by Mr. Larrimer. I felt, rather than saw, Dr. Chapman balk slightly at his designated seat directly opposite Mrs. Larrimer, but I was grateful to know he would be beside me. It seemed he was already acquainted with all but Mr. Fitzgibbons and he finally sat down, after pulling out my mother's chair.

"Miss Shea described to us the rigorous studies you ladies of the university have undertaken, Miss Cabot. We are delighted that you are able to leave your arduous pursuits to join us for such festivities." Mr. Larrimer's charm flowed around me like a warm bath. "We are honored by the presence of two such lovely young ladies who can bring intelligence as well as beauty to our gathering."

I colored at the compliment and expressed my gratitude for the invitation, emphasizing how much I had enjoyed the concert.

"Ah, yes, it was a splendid performance. I must confess, Miss Cabot, I am unlearned in the musical arts. I depend upon Mrs. Larrimer to instruct me in these matters." He turned his gaze on his wife, whose eyes were lowered. "Marguerite is a great lover of music. I am fortunate to be able to depend upon her taste to guide me in opening my spirit to that influence."

There was a pause as I struggled to compose an answer but I was relieved of the responsibility by Mr. Fitzgibbons.

"'That man that hath no music in him, nor is not moved by concord of sweet sounds, is fit for treason, stratagems and spoils.' Thus says the poet Shakespeare, eh, Miss Cabot? But it was a grand concert, was it not? Our symphony orchestra is the pride of our city, Mr. Larrimer. For we would have a great orchestra fit for a city that aspires to greatness."

Mr. Larrimer's concentrated gaze moved from his wife, who still sat with lowered eyes, to the face of the Irishman. He smiled. "And Fitz, here, is our guide to the wonders of your city, Miss Cabot. Why, if we are to believe him, Chicago must be the most amazing city since ancient Greece and Rome."

"We are proud, it is true," Fitzgibbons answered. "How could we not be. Where else in the world could it happen that an entire city could be totally wiped out, destroyed by a mighty blaze, and in only twenty years the inhabitants could rebuild a finer, greater city and execute a marvel such as this great exposition to draw the whole world to us? We are not afraid to boast of it, Mr. Larrimer. No, we are not. And led by your fellow Kentuckian, Mayor Carter Harrison, we have shown the world what a city can be. He's a great man is our mayor and he has asked me to beg you to visit him for some discussion after our repast here tonight."

Mr. Larrimer grinned at this speech and turned once again to me. "You may wonder why Mayor Harrison is so obliging to a poor cotton merchant visiting from the country, Miss Cabot. It seems the mayor would like nothing more than to save the buildings of the White City and to reopen their doors next year so that Chicago may host twice as many visitors who may spend twice as much cash here, I do believe. But to do this requires federal funds and my brother Kentuckian hopes that by some sweet whisperings into the ear of a Kentucky congressman, who just happens to be my first cousin, I might be able to further his plan. Is that not so, Fitz?"

The Irishman was undaunted by this bluntness. "It is true. This world's fair has been a very great success. It has been the greatest educator of the century. The mayor only hopes that Congress will see this great thing and approve the appropriation to continue it for another year. But I cannot describe the plan with the eloquence it deserves, so I only hope you will allow me to bring you to him after supper, so he may convince you himself."

Larrimer laughed. "I do declare, I have never met such out-and-out blatant boosters as these Chicago men. I am sure if that is an example of ineloquence I must surely hear Mayor Harrison's version after dinner."

He signaled a waiter and the service began.

I was happy to be distracted by the necessity of eating, while Mr. Fitzgibbons entertained us with a description of the arduous efforts required in the last mayoral campaign, during which Mr. Harrison had been pitilessly assailed by the local press, in spite of which he had succeeded. Meanwhile, on my right, I could hear Dr. Chapman conversing with Dr. Ramsey.

"And how are your studies, Stephen? Are they living up to your expectations?" Mrs. Larrimer's father had an imposing voice that was pitched low with a full timbre.

"I am privileged to be instructed by some of the finest minds now engaged in the study of biology and chemistry here."

The older man raised an expressive eyebrow. "I confess I cannot see how your studies will progress without affiliation with a teaching hospital. I find your university president's idea that the schools would not be aligned with the practicum of a real medical school to be a very foolish one."

Dr. Chapman appeared to consider this and responded gravely. "It is the belief of President Harper, shared by those of us on the faculties, that medical research has been hampered by too close an association with practical application and the pressures of providing treatment. It is our belief that only by intensive research, free from those restrictions, can we achieve a radical change in medical theory. So much of what is taught now has changed so little since even the Middle Ages."

"And there is good reason for it," Dr. Ramsey objected. "Radical change. You don't know what you are talking about. As I taught you long ago, Stephen, medicine is an art as much as a science. Its traditions are venerable and, you will find in the end, they are inevitable."

Dr. Chapman looked across at him and their gazes locked for a moment. I felt certain they were rehearsing an old argument and

I had a sudden image of them standing in an operating room, with blood on the floor, separated not by a table laden with linens, etched glass and china but by the corpse of some poor soul whose life had been the inevitable sacrifice to the lore of current and past practice. I thought I understood, then, a little of the frustration that must have driven Dr. Chapman to abandon his practice as a surgeon. Marguerite Larrimer seemed also to have been caught up by the discussion and she was looking at my companion with a sort of kindly regret.

"How was your paper received at the medical congress?" Mr. Larrimer interjected this question aimed at his father-in-law and it seemed calculated to emphasize the older man's professional eminence at the expense of Dr. Chapman.

"Very well, I must say. It was very well received." Dr. Ramsey appeared gratified.

"I am in awe of my father-in-law, Miss Cabot. I had no idea when I fell in love with my darling Marguerite that I would be aligning myself with such a famous man."

His wife's eyes were lifted to him as if in pleading, although I did not know why.

"But I have no doubt, Dr. Chapman, you university men must be strong in your devotion to your research. Perhaps, in the end, you will prove the older men wrong."

I expected Dr. Chapman to defend his position with all the fervor of his beliefs but he applied himself to the last of his supper plate as if he had nothing more to say.

"The opportunity to pursue original research is one of the primary goals of the university plan. It is modeled after the German universities in this," I felt obliged to explain.

Mr. Larrimer's attention returned to me and, where it had been sharp when turned on the men in the assembly, I found his attitude always softened when conversing with me. "And are you, too, concerned with chemical experiments, Miss Cabot?"

"Oh, no. Clara—Miss Shea— is, but I study sociology. As a matter of fact," my gaze flickered towards Mr. Fitzgibbons, "I have been compiling a set of statistics on crime in the city. I have had the assistance of the police department in this, in particular a Detective Henry Whitbread."

"Here is an aspect of the city you have not touted, Mr. Fitzgibbons," Larrimer chided him in jest. "Crime in the city and a lady scholar to study it."

"Whitey is it, then, you are working with?" Mr. Fitzgibbons smiled broadly. "He's a wonderful upright man, is Detective Whitbread. And known for his incorruptibility. A fine man. And you will not be holding that against us, Mr. Larrimer. You know very well any city will have the need for a police. It's no more than human nature when you have so many souls in a single place now."

I was going to make a serious comment concerning my research but the two men took command of the conversation at this point.

"And Fitz has not totally ignored this aspect in acting as my guide, Miss Cabot. I must admit he has shown me the Levee as well as the Art Institute."

"There now, that's no topic for the ladies even if they do compile statistics," Mr. Fitzgibbons protested. I was well aware that the Levee was a district notorious for its brothels and gambling halls. "Any great city is going to be composed of many elements good and bad, high and low, and the great achievement is going to be getting them all, if not quite working together, at least not preventing each other. It's a great machine with many wheels and cogs to be kept clear to go round in their own way."

"But there are good elements and bad elements, are there not?" Larrimer asked. "You've had your hands full trying to keep the bad elements under control, we see. All those foreign anarchists have to be kept in check or they'll tear down the carefully oiled machinery of your Northern industrial society, if you're not careful."

A pained expression flashed across Mr. Fitzgibbons face. "It's the Haymarket affair you're thinking of," he said sadly. "That was a black day, a black day for the city. And it shouldn't have happened. It never should have happened. We were there, you know. The mayor rode right up to the podium. Oh, sure, they were spouting blood and glory, death to the capitalists and all that but I tell you, there's many a time I've heard worse and many a time I've heard bloodier. Why, they were going on such a pace we thought for sure we could leave them and they would sputter out with all their rhetoric like a candle at the end of the wick." He shook his head. "So we left and it was a fine mess that followed. I only wish we had stayed. If only we had stayed that day it never would have happened. The mayor could have kept them from rioting, for all that."

"I can't imagine how Harrison could have gotten up at the trial and spoken for those men." Mr. Larrimer shook his head. "I don't know what he was thinking of."

"But, you see, it couldn't have been them that done it," Fitzgibbons protested. "They were up there in full view of the crowd, them that were there at all. We had the police swearing to it even. Whoever threw that bomb it wasn't one of them. And the people knew it. He had to speak up for the people." He settled back in his chair again. "The people knew he spoke for them, and they voted him back in, even after Mr. Marshall Field and all them did their best to be rid of him."

"So, Harrison aligns himself with the dregs of the earth and against the good cultured people of the city?"

"No, no. It's not that way at all. He's a businessman's mayor, it's a city built on business. All I'm saying is the little people must have their place, too. Take the Fair, now. It was the work of our great businessmen. It was their desire to build it and show the world what Chicago can do. But all your little people labored on it and they all have to have their days. So we gave them a German Day and an Irish Day, and like that for all of them." He gestured broadly with one hand. "So, now they can all have their celebration, see? That's the way of it in a place like this, with all these folks from all those different countries all living together like."

Mr. Larrimer sat back as waiters removed the plates. "And a Colored People's Day. The other day when you took us on an excursion to the Pullman factory town, instead of the Fair, that was the Colored People's Day, wasn't it?" He turned to me. "You see, Miss Cabot, Fitz here is very sensitive to our Southern feelings. He thought I would not appreciate such a delicate effort on his part to prevent us from being offended by that Douglass and all. But I do appreciate it, I do."

I had no idea how to respond to this, especially since I was so aware that our waiters were all Negroes. But Mr. Fitzgibbons gave a quick reply.

"Now, then, like I said, we had days for all the different peoples and as there were some who thought Mr. Douglass ought to have had an appointment to the commission, and there were those of your Southern compatriots who would have walked out if any such thing were done, there had to be a little compromise, as you may say."

I had heard of Frederick Douglass, an escaped slave who had spoken against the institution of slavery before the War between the States. I had not heard him mentioned in connection with the Fair before.

"But it seems, despite your efforts, this Douglass has managed to obtain an appointment." Mr. Larrimer raised his eyebrows at Fitzgibbons.

"He was appointed by the Haitian government," Dr. Chapman spoke up calmly. "He served as our ambassador there and it is at the pavilion of that small island nation that he serves. There are many visitors, Negro and white, who seek him out there."

I noticed my mother was listening closely to this exchange. I wondered, for a moment, whether all those tensions between North and South that had resulted in civil war still lay so near the surface as to break out again, even here. I could not understand it. It had all happened before I was even born. But Fitzgibbons interceded.

"Here, now, no sense flogging a dead horse, so to speak. Mr. Douglass is holding court in a tiny house among the foreign countries but we have managed a great fair where arts and industries from all the states are represented. There are those that say it is the greatest joint undertaking between the North and the South since before the war and we have been at great pains to be sure our Southern visitors are comfortable and well taken care of. I'm sure the mayor, himself, would want to make sure that is the case, Mr. Larrimer, if you will only let me take you to him. For, as you know, he is a native of your state and he would like to talk to you about his old home and other things."

"Other things including the need for the federal appropriation, I am sure. But if the ladies can spare us, I believe you may take me to Harrison. And I will have to thank him heartily for providing us with such an amusing and gallant guide."

They excused themselves and moved from the table. Others were also rising and I found Clara and Alden beside me.

"Come on, Em," my brother said, pulling at my chair. "We want to explore. Someone told us they are resetting the hall for dancing."

I excused myself and Clara and I followed him out into the high-ceilinged hall where a dance floor had been cleared.

"What did you think of Mr. Larrimer?" Clara asked me as Alden slipped on ahead.

"He was very charming."

"Oh, yes, he has the charm of a Southern gentleman. But he has a most mercurial temperament, it is said. My father claims he is a hard man in business. He says it is because after the war his home was in ruins and all his male relatives were dead. He had to struggle to keep a roof over the heads of his mother and sisters."

We were following Alden as he threaded his way through the crowd to where a small group of musicians were tuning their instruments.

"Look, Clara. Isn't that Michel Langlois?"

The handsome Frenchman was a violinist in the Chicago Orchestra. We made his acquaintance the previous spring. Just as I recognized the musician, he also saw us and, balancing his violin on a chair, he came to greet us.

"Miss Cabot, Miss Shea, but it is wonderful to see you."

We introduced Alden and were exchanging news of our doings during the summer when suddenly Michel looked beyond me and exclaimed, "C'est la!" and he continued on in his native tongue, talking over my shoulder.

I looked around and saw a young Negro waiter who stood in the shadows beside a door.

"Pardonnez-moi." Michel rushed over to embrace the young man.

They conversed in French, the young Negro man speaking fluently, as far as I could tell.

"Oh, dear," said Clara, but he gestured for us to join him and insisted on introducing his friend.

"This is Roland Johnson. He is a fine violinist. He has studied with the great Dvořák who is teaching now in New York."

He was a tall, straight-backed young man who bowed stiffly from the waist and looked as if he doubted the wisdom of his friend's enthusiasm in accosting him so openly. But Michel launched into another assault of rapid French and I was both amused and relieved by his disregard for local prejudices that would have prevented such an exchange, if he had understood them. Clara, who understood French quite well, became very quiet, while Alden looked like he was about to interrupt, whether or not he understood the conversation.

I was going to suggest we leave them, when I noticed Roland stiffen and I followed his gaze across the room to where Mr. Larrimer stood in a group that included Mayor Carter Harrison and his representative, Mr. Fitzgibbons. It was a look of mutual shock and surprise, although the young Negro man quickly turned his gaze back to Michel. Mr. Larrimer, on the other hand concentrated a stare in our direction and I could see a flicker as he recognized Clara and me. I saw him turn sharply and murmur something to Fitzgibbons. It was then that I remembered the young Negro who had approached Marguerite Larrimer at the Fair. When I looked again at Roland Johnson it seemed to me he might have been the same man.

The thought was somehow uncomfortable and I looked back at the Mayor's group where I noticed a thin man wearing an evening coat a size too large for him break away to approach us. I had the impression he had been dispatched by Mr. Fitzgibbons. I watched him walk to the conductor and speak to him. A moment later, Michel's chatter was interrupted by the sharp rap of a baton on a music stand.

"Mr. Langlois, if you please." The conductor was calling him.

"Excuse me. We must no longer keep these lovely ladies from the dance floor and I must do my part."

With a final flurry of French aimed at Roland, he returned to the platform leaving us somewhat awkwardly placed in conversation with the young waiter. It was a fact that did not greatly disturb my brother or me but seemed to make Clara uncomfortable. Alden wished the young man a jaunty good evening and turned to persuade my friend to dance with him.

Then, just as we were moving away, I saw the thin man who had left the mayor's party put a heavy hand on Roland's shoulder and whisper in his ear. I stopped a few feet away feeling oddly apprehensive and almost wondering if I ought to interfere. A look of anger showed for the briefest moment on the young man's features but with a great effort he mastered it and, lowering his eyes, he turned to walk away, shaking off the other man's hand. I felt compelled to follow him but suddenly found Mr. Fitzgibbons in front of me.

"Miss Cabot, will you do me the honor of this dance?"

Here was another surprise. It seemed to me that, except for Roland, the Irishman was the last man of my acquaintance in the room from whom I would have expected the request.

But the music was starting and before I knew it I found myself being led to the floor where a waltz was beginning.

"Who was that man?" I asked, looking back at the departing figures. He glanced briefly in that direction and stopped.

"Patrick Eugene Prendergast. Like many others he supported the mayor in the last election so he has expectations of a position. But he won't settle down and be satisfied with the job he was given. He's a man with a mission. He has a plan for getting the trains to run on elevated platforms without costing anyone any money—not the train people and not the city. He says if he can only get the appointment he can be the savior of us all and he's a hard man to escape, if you'll believe me. But that's the way of it, you see. The mayor is besieged by men with ambitions like Prendergast. I try to keep him in check. But, come, the music is starting."

Then I was distracted by the need to join the swaying dance. Mr. Fitzgibbons was an unexpectedly good dancer who led firmly and seemed only to be restraining himself from a more vigorous version of the waltz as we whirled around to the music. He sensed my surprise and began to entertain me with stories of dances held with great regularity in the Irish neighborhoods of the city. It was a part of society alien to me. But, in my new position as a student of social structures, every level and layer of society was of interest to me. And as a researcher I had found in the past year that I was free to investigate in the name of my studies—freer than I ever would have imagined. So I listened to the Irishman, as if taking notes for my research.

When the music ended, I found he had whirled me to a place safely beside my brother and Clara, where he made a graceful bow, to which I returned my best curtsy. With a word of thanks, he left me.

Clara was overwhelmed. "Mr. Fitzgibbons! Somehow I never would have expected him to be a dancer," she whispered. "But where is Dr. Chapman, Emily?"

We looked around and saw that most of our party had come out into the hall. My mother and Clara's grandmother found seats, while most of the others were walking along the sides, but we could not see the doctor. Alden slipped away in pursuit of the Irishman. And Clara was engaged to dance at once by one of her many cousins. I told her I would go in search of the doctor since we both felt we should not abandon him.

Thinking he might have remained at the supper table, I found my way back through the crowd. The music was just starting again when I reached the doorway.

Alone inside, Marguerite Larrimer and Dr. Chapman sat together in what appeared to be an intimate conversation. To my dismay I realized I had burst in on them without warning. She had tears streaming down her beautiful face and he held her hands in both of his, head bowed over them. There was a good deal of pain in his eyes when he raised them to me and a good deal of bleakness. Although both looked up at my entrance, they seemed hard put to return from whatever scene they had been playing to register my presence. I felt appalled to have come upon them like that as if I had broken in on a scene of great grief. It was almost like a physical presence, pushing back at me and the only thing I could think of was when I had come upon my mother kneeling by the corpse of my father at his wake. But I sensed I must appear to them like a child who has broken in on a grownup conversation and it vexed me. Somehow Marguerite Larrimer always made me feel childish by comparison.

"Oh, excuse me. I am so sorry," I mumbled and turning on my heel, I escaped.

FOUR

I felt breathless making my way back through the crowd again, so when I saw a doorway I was grateful to find it led out into the warm evening air. On the steps of the building I found a corner where I could lean on a low stone wall, overlooking the peaceful water of the Basin. It was quiet. The sounds of the crowd and the music were muted behind me and the entire Court of Honor lay before me lit up by electric lights. I stood for some minutes with all the scenes of the evening flashing through my mind in a jumble while I watched helplessly. I was still feeling confused, but somewhat more composed, when I heard a voice behind me.

"Miss Cabot."

I turned and saw Dr. Chapman standing in the shadows a few yards away.

"I am so sorry for surprising you like that," I said impulsively.

"Please allow me to explain," he said, moving closer.

"It is not necessary," I said with a gesture and turned back to view the Basin. "It was my mistake. You do not need to explain."

He was silent for a moment, then continued gravely. "Miss Cabot, you came upon me and Mrs. Larrimer in what might be considered a compromising situation. You know only that you have witnessed an emotional confrontation between a single man and a woman who is married to someone else. I beg you to allow me to explain."

I was amazed that he should think he needed to explain himself to me. He apparently feared that I would misinterpret what I had seen. Did he really believe I had rushed off to tattle to my mother and the others? I felt like I could have railed at him had he not seemed at that moment so distant and so formal.

"As you wish," I managed to say stiffly.

"You cannot be aware that at one time, some years ago now, Mrs. Larrimer and I were betrothed." I willed myself not to flinch and remembered suddenly that Clara had told me the doctor had once been engaged and his fiancée had broken it off. This information was much more private than anything he had ever told me about himself. I knew the propriety of the situation was questionable but I was not going to try to stop him. No longer stuck in the tiny restricted social world where I grew up, now I was a member of the university community and Dr. Chapman was a colleague and friend. "I was a student and protégé of her father. Through him we met and formed an attachment. Marguerite was young then. She was full of hope and enthusiasm and plans, very like you and Miss Shea. Her father did not approve of the match. She was his only child and he knew that I had neither fortune nor family connections. Marguerite had been raised in luxury and loved music, which she studied at that time. Her father wanted to spare her a life of penury, which he knew was all I could hope to offer. When she was adamant, he even offered to help set me up with a share of his very lucrative medical practice among the wealthy of Baltimore.

"But I was proud and stubborn and young. I had grown up in the slums of Baltimore as the son of a traveling preacher. Having lived among the poor as my father ministered to their souls, I was determined to do a better job of improving their lot by ministering to their bodies. My father always objected to my profession and Marguerite's father objected to the social and financial status of my patients. But I was arrogant and wanted to prove both of them wrong. So when I broke from her father, I insisted on releasing Marguerite from the engagement. In my youthful pride I was sure her devotion to me would be as strong as my own determination to follow my chosen fate.

"Of course, it was a foolish assumption that could only be made by a very proud, very young person. I have no doubt she must have felt abandoned by me. So when her father introduced her to the older, wealthier Mr. Charles Larrimer, how could she not be gratified by his obvious admiration, and his intense Southern charm? She has always been exquisite to look at, in addition to having an acute intelligence and an innocent purity of heart that everything in her sheltered upbringing had sought to maintain. It was an immense shock to me when she accepted him and it was with barely concealed satisfaction that her father extended an invitation to me to attend the wedding. I am quite sure he considered that he had taught me one final lesson. We parted on seemingly friendly terms, the couple moving away to Larrimer's home in Kentucky."

He paused for a moment but I had nothing to say.

"In addition to this . . . disappointment . . . I soon found my ambitions to right the wrongs of the world by providing medical treatment were fruitless. No matter how many beds you provide for the sick, no matter how many hours you spend in surgery, the final numbers of those who live and those who die remain little affected. I finally realized that until we could know more about the causes of disease, there could be no impact on the numbers affected. I saw that all the energy I was expending on treatment was wasted and finally I decided to turn from that to research. I began work at a laboratory at Johns Hopkins and slowly withdrew from my regular practice.

"It was at that time, when I had still not determined exactly what course of study to pursue, that I happened to take a trip that took me close to the Larrimer estate. With some misgivings, I decided nonetheless that it would be perfectly proper for me to pay a visit to Marguerite. Since I had had to admit I had been wrong in my own original plans, I wondered what had become of her. I suspected that, unlike me, she had been wise in her choices.

"I was sorely disappointed. Mr. and Mrs. Larrimer received me graciously but it was obvious to me that hers was not a happy marriage. Despite every physical comfort she led a miserable existence. Contrary to what you may think, based on a slight acquaintance, he is a cruel man despite his apparent charm. Poor Marguerite was no happier in her choice than I was."

He paused again as if deciding how much to tell me. "I cannot relate the details but can only say that it was an unhappy visit that ended unhappily. I was in no position to offer Marguerite any assistance and I soon departed as I could not bear to see her in that situation. You are too young to know how it feels to see someone you had known, when all the world was before them, mired down by the choices they have made in life. There is nothing you can do for them. It is too late." He paused as if deciding how to continue.

"After I left, she suffered a most terrible experience that I am not at liberty to share with you. But it was that which she was describing to me this evening and it was that which provoked the emotion you witnessed. It is only because she has known me for such a very long time and in such peculiar circumstances that she has confided in me in this way. And I must beg you to understand and not to judge either of us too hastily."

I strained to see his face but he was shrouded in darkness. There was a gulf between us wider than the few feet of stone. I felt then the ten years difference in our ages much more than I had done since we had met. When I had first become acquainted with the doctor, during the invigorating opening days of the university, we had all seemed comrades in a new adventure, but I realized now, that he was really a stranger about whom I knew very little. But he was still my friend.

"I am very sorry to hear of such unhappiness," I said somewhat inadequately. "I would not presume to judge you or Mrs. Larrimer and I do assure you I will not betray your confidence. Are we not friends, Doctor? Am I not in your debt, even? Whatever may have happened in the past, I could not think badly of you. You must know that."

My words dropped into the night air and were followed by a deep silence marred only by the muffled sounds from inside the building. I could not see his face to judge his reaction.

"You are too generous. You must excuse me, Miss Cabot. Please make my excuses to your mother."

He disappeared before I could make any reply and it was with some sadness that I saw his back fading away up the promenade a moment later. I had the unhappy impression that I had lost something and that our relations could never again be as free and confident as they had been in the past. He was never an easy man to know but I had come to feel close to him, nonetheless. I felt that closeness sundered by this episode although I could not understand why it should be so.

With heavy feelings I reentered the hall in search of my mother. She, too, was ready to return to our lodgings but she informed me that Alden had plans to visit the Midway with Mr. Fitzgibbons. The Irishman gave me a considering look as he stood across from me with Alden and Mr. Larrimer. Mrs. Larrimer sat by my mother. She was composed and regal once again and after a single anxious glance at me, she seemed relieved, looking, as always, very beautiful. Hearing that we wished to depart, she soon arranged to offer us a ride in their carriage as the Sheas were still dancing and did not propose to leave yet.

So it was that we found ourselves in the company of the Larrimers and Dr. Ramsey, being driven through the mild evening air in their spacious carriage. We gave the coachman directions and settled back. I was very quiet not knowing what to think of these people after all I had heard that evening. Mr. Larrimer responded to my mother's profuse thanks.

"We are delighted to be able to escort you lovely ladies home," he told us. "We can only consider it a privilege and opportunity lost to your male companions who would abandon such beauty and grace for the rough amusements of the Midway."

"I'm afraid my son was terribly anxious to be able to visit the Midway with Mr. Fitzgibbons," my mother said. "He is full of curiosity about the place."

"Have no fear, Mrs. Cabot. The Irishman will take care of him. If he would visit such treacherous amusements it is well he is under the care of such a man wise in the ways of the world. But it is the error of youth to think such common things more attractive than the beauty of a warm summer night in the company of the gentle sex."

We were glad to finally reach our rooms. As we prepared for bed I was distracted from my musings by an unexpected request from my mother. Thus far she had been content to allow me to make all of the plans for what we would visit in our tour of the Fair. But now she announced that she very much wished to visit the Haitian pavilion.

"I should like to pay my respects to Mr. Douglass," she said firmly. "At one time your father assisted him with some legal matters. He may not recall it but I feel sure if your father were here he would want to meet him and shake his hand."

FIVE

*T*he next morning we collected Alden from the men's dormitory and stopped at the Liberal Arts building where I was able to arrange for a substitute to cover my post. Alden had persuaded Clara to meet us at the Ferris Wheel in the afternoon, so the morning was devoted to finding the Haitian pavilion and paying our respects to Mr. Douglass, as my mother wished.

Separate structures built by foreign governments were located in the northern part of the fairgrounds. We passed over a bridge, with Wooded Island to our left, and skirted around the Fisheries Building to the collection of smaller buildings each done in the style of their home country. There we found the Haitian pavilion on a corner opposite the curious turrets of the Swedish building and the small exotic palace that represented East India.

Flags snapped in a brisk lake breeze from poles that supported an ornate pediment painted white with gold decoration. It was mounted over the entrance on pairs of columns decorated with flares of golden birds. Shorter columns supported the roof of a deep porch that wrapped around the building and a golden cupola rose up behind the triangle of the pediment.

As we mounted the short flight of steps, Dr. Chapman came out of the large open doors.

"Miss Cabot, Alden, Mrs. Cabot. Good morning." He was surprised to see us. My mother stepped forward.

"Good morning, Doctor. We have come in hopes of seeing Mr. Douglass. I am happy to see you. I was sorry we were not able to wish you good evening last night."

"I do apologize. I should have seen you home."

"Oh, no. We were well taken care of. Emily told us you had left." He gave me a worried look, but my mother continued placidly. "We did not have nearly enough conversation, however. I wonder if you would be so good as to join us for tea this afternoon, at our lodgings."

He hesitated for only a moment. "I would be most obliged." Then he grinned. It was as if he had shed some burden that he had been struggling under the previous night. I could not understand the change in his attitude.

"Good. Five o'clock then? We will not keep you this morning, as I am sure you must be busy. But we will look forward to seeing you then."

He bowed and left as we turned into the building.

I was too surprised by my mother's sudden invitation to attempt to forestall her, but as we walked down the short corridor I decided it was a good thing and could only help to demonstrate to him that I had not betrayed his confidences of the previous evening—if he even came. In any case, whatever awkwardness might remain from the memory of that conversation, it would be more easily overcome by such a meeting.

The corridor ended in a large round room lit by the clerestory of the building's cupola. A mosaic floor represented the bird which must be a symbol of the Haitian republic and there was a crowd of people, colored and white, strolling into adjoining rooms or waiting on plush benches around the sides. We headed towards a raised wooden desk where a young Negro woman appeared to be greeting visitors.

Petite with large dark eyes and an open expression, she wore a fine day gown in shades of green with darker frogging that set off her very dark complexion to advantage. She spoke with great animation to each group that approached. As we came closer I realized she was perched on a high stool, and beside her was a lower table piled with pamphlets bound in red boards that she was offering to the people she greeted. We waited until she turned to us and then my mother spoke up.

"Good morning."

"Good morning. I am Ida B. Wells. Welcome to the Haitian exhibit. Can I ask you to read our pamphlet?" She held out one of the red colored books. As I stepped forward and took it for my mother, I saw the title was *The Reason Why the Colored American Is Not in the World's Columbian Exposition*. "It is a clear, plain statement of the facts concerning the oppression put upon colored people in this land of the free and home of the brave."

As I looked up at her, I became aware of a tall prosperous looking colored man leaning against a column behind her. He seemed aware that I was a little startled by this presentation and he, himself, seemed to be admiring the effect of Miss Wells's speech with a certain sardonic amusement. My mother was unshaken from her goal.

"Thank you, my dear. We will be sure to read it with attention. I am Mrs. Catherine Cabot and this is my daughter, Emily, and my son, Alden. My deceased husband, Mr. John Cabot, had the privilege of working with Mr. Frederick Douglass some years ago. I was wondering if it might be possible for us to greet Mr. Douglass and pay our respects."

Miss Wells seemed very gratified by the request. "I am sure Mr. Douglass will be most anxious to see you. Every day he has received a great many visitors who want to shake his hand or remember some instance of anti-slavery agitation in which they or their parents took part. He is extremely grateful for these attentions. I believe he is engaged in several such meetings even as we speak but, if you would not mind waiting, I will be more than happy to let him know that you are here."

"I would greatly appreciate that."

"I am sorry you have to wait, but if you would like to take a seat, I will send someone to take you to him as soon as possible." She gestured at the plush-covered benches.

"Thank you very much, my dear. We will be happy to wait."

As we found seats I saw Miss Wells scribble a note which she handed to the tall man behind her, waving him away with a smile. Then she turned to the next couple and, handing them a copy of the pamphlet, I could see she was prepared to arrange a similar meeting for them. As I looked around I realized there were a number of people, some colored, some white, who must have come on similar errands and I was impressed by this desire to meet the great man. Soon Alden wandered off to look at the exhibits in other rooms but I remained to keep my mother company, and I was idly beginning to read the pamphlet which contained essays by several people, including Miss Wells, when my attention was drawn to the center of the round mosaic floor.

Miss Wells had climbed down from her stool and was leading a young Negro man, who had a violin under his arm, to the center. I recognized him as Roland Johnson, the friend of Mr. Langlois. Now I was sure this was the same young man I had seen talking to Mrs. Larrimer in the Manufactures Building. He looked much more self-assured in a suit and tie and when he noticed me he bowed slightly. I returned the acknowledgement as best I could from my seated position.

"Ladies and gentlemen, Mr. Douglass wishes me to apologize to any of you who are waiting to see him and we would like to make the delay pleasanter by asking Mr. Roland Johnson to entertain you. Mr. Johnson is a very fine musician who has studied in Europe and we have asked him to play for you today."

This announcement was greeted with applause and soon all of our attention was captured by the performance. He played expertly and I soon realized he was playing a part of the theme from *Scheherazade*, which we had heard the night before. There was silence as the plaintive notes rose up into the lofty ceiling, while the musician played with a look of total concentration. Once again I was drawn into that exotic world of the imagination, a place so fascinating I felt a slight reluctance to leave when Miss Wells quietly signaled us to follow her for our meeting. Even Alden, who had been drawn back to the main room by the music, joined us. She led us down some corridors to a pleasant sitting room with French doors open to a fragrant garden full of late blooming flowers.

Mr. Frederick Douglass was a medium-sized man in his seventies with a quiet manner but a great presence nonetheless. He had a mane of frizzy graying hair, a full beard and deep brown eyes in a face lined by years but very benevolent in aspect. Taking both my mother's hands in his, he greeted her warmly.

"My dear Mrs. Cabot, I cannot tell you how gratified I am to meet you and how sorry I am to hear that your husband is no longer with us. Please accept my deepest sympathies. It is a great loss for us all."

I saw tears in my mother's eyes but she thanked him and presented me and Alden.

"Your father was of very great help to me and others in our struggles many years ago," Mr. Douglass told me. "He never hesitated to lend his assistance in legal matters. Many times there was need for expertise that we could never have afforded without the generosity of your father and others like him," he told us, then turned back to my mother. "But time goes on and robs us of our most steadfast friends. I can share your grief, Mrs. Cabot, as

I, too, have lost a dear wife of more than forty years and a son. It is a very hard thing to have to continue without them." He sighed.

"I am so very sorry to hear that, Mr. Douglass," said my mother as she patted his arm. It struck me there was something almost childlike about their grief and I was shocked. For so long the older generation had seemed so unshakeable in their control over life, yet at the moment they both appeared helpless in a way that I had never imagined. Mr. Douglass sighed again and looked into my mother's eyes.

"It was difficult to go on then. I feel you know what I mean." She nodded. "After my son died, I fell into a depression. I would not be consoled." He gave a small smile. "I confess Miss Wells with all her youthful indignation . . . she and her friends have helped to rouse me. But it is difficult, always difficult. But, please sit with me for a little while at least and tell me more. What was it that took Mr. Cabot? Was it illness, as with my dear Anna?"

No, it wasn't illness. My father was murdered, shot by the brother of a man whose case was before him. I could not bear to hear the act described again.

"Excuse me, Mother, but surely there must be others waiting to see Mr. Douglass. Perhaps we should not take up so much of his time." I was ashamed of myself as soon as I said it, and feeling the searching gaze of the great man on me, I lowered my eyes. But my mother reached out and put a hand on my arm.

"You are right, Emily. But I will stay a little longer with Mr. Douglass all the same. Why don't you and Alden wait for me back in the hall? I won't be long."

Mr. Douglass let us go graciously, no doubt sensing my discomfort. We left them together and Alden led me back to the hall then wandered off again. The musician had gone and I found a seat near Miss Wells where I hoped my mother would be sure to find me. I was ashamed of myself but I just did not want to dwell on the details of my father's death yet again. It was a painful time that I had tried to put behind me. To distract myself, as I waited, I began reading the pamphlet I still held in my hand. Soon my attention was more completely distracted from my own remembered grief than I would ever have thought possible.

I skimmed the first several essays devoted to statistics and complaints that, while colored people contributed such a large proportion of labor in this country, their efforts went unrecognized. Then I came upon the chapter concerning lynch law. This was a most disturbing piece and I was amazed to find it had been written by Miss Wells herself. It described in the most lurid and awful detail the lynching of Negroes that had taken place in recent years. One had happened only the previous July in Kentucky, while so many visitors from around the country and the world were viewing all the exhibits demonstrating our country's progress at the Columbian Exposition. A colored man had been arrested for a heinous crime but, before a trial could be held, he was seized and killed and his body desecrated by a lawless crowd. The action was brutal and, as the essay explained, there was reason to believe the wrong man had been accused.

I closed the booklet and realized that I was being observed by both Miss Wells and the prosperous looking man who stood behind her. I looked away. Miss Wells seemed about to descend to speak with me but, just then my mother returned on Alden's arm and we made our departure.

As we came out into the sunshine my mind was full of the dreadful images from the pamphlet, which I still held in my hand, while Alden prattled on about the Ferris Wheel. My mother announced that she would not accompany us to the rendezvous with Clara and her cousins but would return to our lodgings for a rest. She looked pale and I knew her reminiscences with Mr. Douglass had brought back memories of my father. She was sad but assured me she was fine and, reminding me of our appointment for tea with Dr. Chapman, she insisted on walking back alone.

I hid the pamphlet in my skirts. It seemed to me that she would want to read it but, as it was not likely to restore her spirits, I was determined to keep it from her until a better time. So I found myself walking through the crowded amusements of the Midway with no place to put the red pamphlet except to keep it in my hand where it appeared to me to be a burning rebuke to the frivolities of the park. I would have liked nothing better than to have gone home quietly with my mother but the appointment with Clara must be kept.

SIX

*A*lden led the way into the Midway Plaisance and down the long wide avenue towards the Ferris Wheel, which loomed up in the middle. It was a park full of amusements that had become extremely popular with those whom I thought of at that time as the uneducated. The buildings were flimsy affairs, gaudy with signs, some mere shacks. They claimed to represent various cultures and so appealed to the local immigrant workers, many of whom would not pay the price of admission to the Exposition itself. Like my brother, Alden, they had more of a thirst for the beverages served on the Midway than for the knowledge I thought I was getting from the great exhibits of the Fair.

We passed the Irish village with its five-story brick building boldly claiming to be Blarney Castle and the Old Vienna exhibit which represented a street from that city. Throngs of working-class people lined up to pay the twenty-five cents admission fee for these fake streets that housed shops and restaurants. I suppose they found nostalgically familiar things from the homes they had left behind in the Old World and that was more attractive to them than the displays of what we thought was progress and culture in the main buildings.

As we neared the huge wheel Alden pointed out the minarets of the Street in Cairo exhibit with enthusiasm, but I was just as impressed by the tawdriness of the area as I had been in the past. Yet I was always in awe of the great web of steel girders that made up the Ferris Wheel itself and I craned my neck now to look up at it. Alden rushed off to find some acquaintance he had made the previous evening, leaving me to wait for Clara and her party. I was so amazed by the sight I nearly walked into a man whose sudden cough broke into my reverie.

"Ah, Miss Cabot. Good afternoon."

It was the distinguished Dr. Ramsey who seemed out of place, standing near an opening in the wall that surrounded the Ferris Wheel.

"Oh, Dr. Ramsey, how do you do? I am here with my brother to meet Clara and some of her cousins to ride the Ferris Wheel."

Somehow he did not appear happy to hear this news. He shifted uneasily and I noticed him glance at the red pamphlet in my hand and make a cluck of distaste. I shoved it into my skirts behind my back.

"Have you come to ride it also?"

"I am waiting for Charles—Mr. Larrimer. We have business elsewhere."

I was trying to think of topics that would be appropriate to discuss with this haughty man in such an unlikely place, when I was saved the trouble by the appearance of Clara surrounded by three of her male cousins. They greeted us and jabbered on about the camel they had ridden in the Street in Cairo.

Soon after, Mr. Larrimer came through the opening in the wall and joined us. He was asked about the ride. "I did not ride it," he said, giving the huge Ferris Wheel a dismissive glance and pulling on his gloves, which he proceeded to button with care. "I was discharging a debt. You must always remember that debts are a matter of honor." He was addressing the young men of the group. "A man's honor demands they be paid or his reputation will be damaged. Honor is the first concern of a gentleman. Never forget it."

Dr. Ramsey looked even more uncomfortable and I wondered at Mr. Larrimer's pronouncement. It seemed to me an embarrassment even to have incurred the type of debt that he mentioned. That he should trumpet the fact in such a way was surprising. Dr. Ramsey must have thought so too, because he murmured in his son-in-law's ear and they took their leave.

A few minutes later Alden came out through the opening in the wall, followed by a portly man with very black hair wearing a black suit with a plaid vest, and a black top hat. He had a huge black moustache with waxed tips.

"Emily, Clara, Bob, John, Trip, meet Marco, the entrepreneur extraordinaire. He's going to get us on the Wheel."

"Alden . . . your manners. Introduce us properly. I am Miss Emily Cabot, Mister . . . ?"

Alden laughed. "If you mean Marco's surname, Em, you couldn't pronounce it."

I was embarrassed and angry with my brother but the entrepreneur had a twinkle in his eyes as he swept off the top hat and gave us a formal bow.

"Alas, Miss Cabot, it is only too true. To those not trained in the tongue of my birthplace, the syllables of my patronymic present an implacable obstacle. In London, where I was raised, and elsewhere around the globe where I have traveled, I am known simply as— Marco." He had a booming bass voice that was encompassing and an educated British accent. He ended many of his sentences with a deep laugh and he added now, "But you may call me Mr. Marco, if you prefer it."

"Marco will get us on the Wheel. We arranged it last night," Alden told us with pride.

"Indeed, ladies and gentlemen, you have before you the wonder of this fair." Marco gestured and we all looked up at the massive steel structure that soared above us. "Two hundred and fifty feet in diameter, this magnificent structure is named for George W. Ferris, a master bridge builder who designed and constructed it. The forty-five foot long axle is the largest single piece of steel to have been forged in the entire world. There are thirty-six luxurious cars each able to hold sixty people, forty of them seated in absolute comfort on magnificent swivel chairs. Here, my friends, is the marvel of modern scientific construction, and you will not be able to say you have truly seen the Columbian Exposition until you have seen it from this bird's-eye view two hundred and sixty-four feet in the air at the top. You will be amazed, I assure you."

At that moment a thin young man in a checkered suit and a top hat skipped up and grabbed Marco by his coat sleeve.

"Got 'em, mate, and he's ready to come to terms." He had a thick Cockney accent. Marco hushed him but nodded at the man who followed behind. I saw it was Mr. Weaver in his broad-brimmed hat and black clothes. A Westerner, whose exact origins and former employment were unknown, he had a reputation as a dangerous man and it was said that he was hired by the wealthy to do what they would never do themselves. I had witnessed him hold a pistol to the head of a man once, in an attempt to intimidate him. He noticed me now and, to my discomfort, he touched his hat as a sign of recognition. I exchanged a glance with Clara and as if by agreement we turned away, ignoring him. Marco clapped the younger man on the back and introduced him.

"And here is my associate, Mr. Teddy Hanover. But let us wait no longer. Teddy will take you all in and get you on the first available car. This way, ladies and gentlemen. I promise, you won't be disappointed."

As Marco and Teddy began herding us in through the opening in the wall, I noticed the booth advertising a fifty cents admission price.

"But, shouldn't we purchase tickets?" I asked, bringing out my reticule. I felt Weaver's eyes on me from behind.

"Put it away. Put it away, dear lady," Marco told me. "For friends of Fitz no admission fee and the best seats in the house." Alden gave me a satisfied grin and Marco told me confidentially,

"No, no, Miss Cabot, we must keep on the right side of the city, you know. We are always happy to oblige the mayor's representative in these matters. It's all arranged, not to worry. Teddy, get them on the next car and give them the first class tour."

So we all followed the young man and soon found ourselves being wafted aloft in a huge glassed-in car with red plush swivel seats. Despite a waiting line of people, our party had a car all to itself.

I sat down with a plop and experienced the very strange feeling of being lifted into the air. We faced outward and all the machinery was behind us so we seemed to be suspended as if by magic. It was a little unsettling. But, as with everything, we soon took it for granted and listened as Teddy rattled on with his speech by rote, detailing the wonders to be seen below.

At the top we all moved to seats on the other side of the car so as to be on the outside again on the way back down. As I found a place beside Clara I noticed she was staring at the red pamphlet, which I still held, having no place to stow it out of sight.

"What is that?"

I explained about our morning visit to the Haitian pavilion. The others were being entertained by Teddy's patter and we conversed softly. I offered Clara the pamphlet but she held her hands up in protest.

"Oh, no. So that is it. You have no idea what a fuss there was about that. Marguerite Larrimer had a copy and when her husband found it he was furious. There was a huge argument. Well, mainly it was him shouting. He was so angry. And he called in Mr. Fitzgibbons and harangued him about what a disgrace it was to allow such lies to be distributed at the Fair. He told him if they wanted to keep the Fair open they'd pretty well better suppress it. I've never seen a man so angry."

At that moment Teddy called us all over to the windows to enumerate and recommend the Midway exhibits. Surprised by Clara's reaction, I was not paying much attention. My eye wandered as we moved closer to the ground and people who had been mere specks a few minutes before became recognizable. Suddenly I glimpsed Dr. Chapman walking with a lady. Her face was obscured by her parasol but I had no doubt as to who it was. Then we were on the way up the other side, in our second revolution, and we moved back to the plush seats.

I looked down at the red pamphlet in my lap again. Teddy was declaiming to a group who stood by the windows but Clara sat down beside me.

"But, Clara, have you read this yourself? It describes a very great injustice done just this last July in Kentucky. I was very shocked. Surely you must be shocked that such a horrible thing could happen in your own state."

I heard a sharp intake of breath from my friend. "You would condemn us all on such a charge?"

"But I do not . . ."

"You are like all Northerners, Emily. You'll believe any vicious lies you hear. There was a terrible riot last July but do you know what caused it? Two young white girls had their throats slit. They were twelve and thirteen years old, for heavens sake. Can you not see how such a horrible crime would drive the people mad with fear and anger? Do you think Chicago, with its slums and tenements and labor riots, is so virtuous as to condemn us? But it is always the same. You have no idea of the trials and troubles left in the South, no idea at all. You shouldn't spread lies, Emily." She tapped the pamphlet in my lap and, rising, she moved to the group around Teddy.

I was stunned. I looked at the red pamphlet in my lap. It stood out like a blister. There was nothing I could do about it and Clara was right, I knew very little of the circumstances it described. Clara was my friend. I knew her to be a good person. I kept my seat. This was no time to pursue such a discussion and I felt the afternoon was spoiled and longed to have it end.

Soon enough we completed the second rotation and filed out of the car with Clara leading the way and me bringing up the rear. Alden was suggesting a further expedition, but I noticed Teddy pull him aside and speak into his ear after which my brother seemed content, and even determined, to end the outing. He reminded me we needed to be home in time for tea, while Clara reminded her cousins of a dinner engagement in town and insisted they head for the train. We parted with all the appearance of geniality, but Clara avoided looking at me and we both were aware that a coldness had grown up between us.

Just as Alden and I reached the opening in the wall to return to the thoroughfare I heard a voice I recognized raised in anger. Turning, I caught a glimpse of Mr. Fitzgibbons facing Marco. The Irishman wore a bowler hat and dark woolen suit just as I had imagined. He did not see us and I turned away wondering why he was haranguing the entrepreneur like that. On the way out we came upon the thin figure of Mr. Prendergast leaning against the wall. Alden and I exchanged a glance, then nodding to the man, we moved hurriedly into the crowd.

"That Prendergast is an odd duck," my brother told me as we walked. "He sticks to Fitz like a barnacle." It was obvious that Alden was very impressed by Mr. Fitzgibbons. "Hardly ever talks, but he'd do anything for Fitz. No, it's true, Emily. It's a kind of loyalty born of political parties. He's expecting an appointment to some kind of big job in the near future. He did say that much."

Knowing my brother's easy manners and insistent curiosity about people, I was surprised that he had managed to find out so little about the man. About Fitz he had told us a life story—how the man had emigrated with his family, and become the head of it when his father died, and how he had come to support Carter Harrison as a local ward boss in his earliest campaign and so forth. Apparently Mr. Prendergast, unlike his boss Fitzgibbons, was able to keep his peace even after an onslaught from my brother. I was a little uneasy about the type of companions Alden was finding in a strange city, but I knew his stay was only temporary so I could only trust he would not come to harm. Soon he would have to return to Boston and his job at my uncle's bank. I had hoped that Dr. Chapman might provide a steadying influence on him while he was here. But none of my own plans were working out those days.

Back at our rooms my mother appeared rested although I could tell she had been weeping. She was calm, now, and had laid out tea in the sitting room. We had agreed that Alden, who was staying in the men's dormitory, would bring Dr. Chapman with him when he came back at five o'clock so it was a surprise when he arrived alone.

"Dr. Chapman sends his regrets. He asked me to apologize but he said that something urgent had come up and he was forced to change his plans."

I gave my brother a sharp look. There was something he wasn't saying. I remembered the glimpse I had had of the doctor walking with a lady and thought bitterly that the change of plans no doubt was caused by some need of Mrs. Larrimer. My mother was obviously disappointed so I tried to make the best of it, pouring the tea and praising the delicacies she had managed to put out. It was too bad of Dr. Chapman to treat us all this way, but after the revelations of the previous evening I told myself it was to be expected. He had not been acting in his normal manner since Mrs. Larrimer had come on the scene.

Alden put himself out to entertain our mother, describing the ride on the Ferris Wheel but soon she appeared rather tired, and, taking the pamphlet which she intended to read, despite my warning about its sad contents, she retreated to her room. Alden immediately became restless.

"I think I must go out again."

"Again? Alden, you can't be meaning to return to the Midway again. I thought even you had had enough for the day."

"I have. It's not that. It's just . . ." His blue eyes stared straight into mine for a moment. "I have to go, Em. Truth to tell, I'm worried about the doctor."

"What?"

He seemed to consider how much to say but after another look at my face he must have decided to confide all. "The doctor was ready to come. I think he was looking forward to it. But we started to walk here and I told him . . . I told him it was a good thing to stay away from the Midway tonight as something is going to happen there." He hurried on, "Teddy told me . . . before we left . . . he took me aside and advised me to get the ladies away before anything happened. He didn't say what or why but he indicated some kind of disturbance was expected and he said it would be better to stay away, especially from the Dahomey Village. You know, that's the one the French put up in the Midway. It's from an African nation they recently conquered and they have a bunch of natives living in huts."

I stared at him, uncomprehending.

"When the doctor heard that, he insisted on going. I tried to dissuade him, Emily, but he insisted. I can only think I didn't make him understand how seriously Teddy advised against being there. I really think he was saying there is danger of bodily harm, someone will get hurt. I feel responsible for not convincing Dr. Chapman to stay away and I really think I should go after him."

He started towards the door. Grabbing my hat and bag I hurried after him.

"What are you doing? You can't come, Emily."

"Hush, Mother will hear us. I can come and I will come." He knew better than to try to stop me.

We closed the door behind us carefully and hurried down the street, Alden arguing all the while, trying to convince me to stay behind, but I was determined.

We trotted back to the Midway and I followed my brother as he threaded his way through the strolling crowds. We were beyond the

Ferris Wheel, heading towards the Fair proper when I started to notice groups of rough looking men standing around or leaning against walls.

At the Dahomey Village Alden tossed coins to the gatekeeper, and as I followed him in I saw the Westerner, Mr. Weaver, hands in his pockets, leaning against the fence. He stared at me from under the hat pulled low over his eyes. With a shiver I caught up with Alden when suddenly we heard a throaty scream. I barely had time to notice the primitive huts and scantily clad Africans as I ran after Alden. He headed unerringly to the source of the commotion, rushing into a hut off in a back corner of the grounds.

Inside it was dark, with only a small amount of light filtering through the grass roof and a flickering lantern hung on the wall. As my eyes became accustomed to the dimness I picked out a figure lying prone on the floor. Another man was kneeling over it, and when he looked up, I recognized Dr. Chapman.

"He's dead."

I took a step closer and saw it was Mr. Larrimer lying there. Blood spread out on his chest, pooling beneath him, and the doctor's hands. There was a sharp stench and smoke hung in the air. A gun had been fired. A gun lay beside the man on the ground.

"Mr. Cabot, find a policeman and bring him here. Hurry."

SEVEN

*W*hat happened?" I asked taking a step forward when we were alone.

"No, stay back. You cannot help him." Dr. Chapman was staring at the face of the dead man, his jaw set. He sat back on his heels with blood-stained hands on his thighs. "He's been shot."

"But who did this?"

At that moment there was a shrill whistle close at hand and then Alden rushed in with two uniformed policemen.

"Here, now, what's happened?" the older one asked.

"He has been shot. He is quite dead. I am a doctor. There is nothing to be done for him." The doctor stood up and the policeman looked back and forth between him and the dead man. More policemen appeared at the door.

The first policeman stepped over to the body. He stooped and picked up the gun by the body. "Is this your gun? Did you shoot him?"

"No, I heard the shot and came in."

"Did you see who did it? Did he shoot himself?" He sniffed at the barrel of the gun.

"No, I didn't see. But he was shot in the back so he did not do it himself. He fell forward on his face. I turned him over to see if I could help him but he was shot in the back."

"Hasn't been fired," the policeman declared about the gun. "It was another gun." He looked around. As other uniformed officers started to enter he stopped them. "It's a shooting. You check the grounds. Look for a man with a gun. Keep everybody out." He waved off most of them and then pointed to one younger officer, "You, Peter, go get the wagon. Have them pull in here, all the way." As the others left on these errands he turned back to the doctor.

"Your name, sir?"

"Stephen Chapman. I am a medical doctor. I am currently enrolled at the University of Chicago and I lodge at a dormitory there. This is Miss Emily Cabot, also a student of the university, and her brother, Alden, who is visiting from Boston."

"And the dead man?"

"Mr. Charles Larrimer of Kentucky."

"Was he a friend of yours then?"

"An acquaintance."

At that moment there was a commotion at the door and Mr. Prendergast came plunging in.

"Here, now. I told them to keep people out," our policeman shouted.

"I'm Eugene Prendergast. I'm with the mayor's office. I work for Fitz." The policeman obviously recognized the name and Prendergast walked over to where the dead man lay. "Do you know who this is?"

"I'm just finding out. You knew him?"

"I do. I saw him come in here. I was waiting outside to see if he needed anything when he came out. This man is a very important visitor. He's Mr. Charles Larrimer from Kentucky. Fitz and I had been escorting him around, seeing to his needs. Harrison is expecting him to help to get the funding to keep the Fair open. This is terrible. The mayor is going to want to know what happened. He was depending on this man. What will he say when he finds out the man was killed, here on the Midway? There's going to be trouble, a lot of trouble. The mayor will be furious."

"Yes, well we're none to happy about it ourselves, Mr. Prendergast. Since you seem to know the man perhaps you can help then. I was just about to ask this gentleman what happened. He says he's a doctor."

"Dr. Stephen Chapman. As I said, I am connected to the university. I knew Charles Larrimer but I did not see what happened. I was in the village when I heard the shot and I came and found him. He was face down. I tried to help him but it was too late."

"You didn't see who fired the shot?"

"No."

"Is that your gun?"

"No, I assumed it was Larrimer's. It was beside him."

"You sure you didn't see anyone?"

"No, I saw him. That's all. It was obvious he needed help. That took all my attention, I'm afraid."

Mr. Prendergast was staring at the doctor with a frown on his face. "I know you," he told him. "I know him." He was pointing at the doctor now but he grabbed the policeman's arm. "He was at the dinner the other night. He knew Larrimer. He knew Larrimer's wife. I heard he was engaged to Larrimer's wife before she married Larrimer. Don't let him go. He must have done it. He shot Larrimer in a jealous fit."

"I did no such thing," the doctor replied sharply.

"You knew him, though, like he says?" the policeman asked. "You were engaged to his wife?"

"Yes, I knew him. This has nothing to do with Mrs. Larrimer. It is many years since I have seen them before the other night. I certainly did not shoot the man."

"But you just happened to be here when he was shot? And who are you two again?" He turned to my brother and me. "Did you come with him?"

At that moment the thought came into my mind that it would be simpler if, as he obviously assumed, all three of us had arrived together. I think Alden had the same idea. One of us might have said something to give that impression if Dr. Chapman had not spoken first.

"No. We came separately. I heard the shot and found him. Miss Cabot and her brother came in a few moments later."

I nodded. While the policeman asked for our names and addresses, Mr. Prendergast was shaking his head and repeating to himself, "This is terrible, just terrible. This is terrible." He grabbed the arm of the officer again. "Do you know what this means to the mayor? He is going to want to know what happened. To think that Larrimer was shot at the Fair. How will that look? How will we ever get Congress to pass the appropriations bill now? When they hear about this, what do you think they will do? Arrest that man. You must arrest that man."

"No. You can't do that," I protested. I could see Prendergast was making the policeman very nervous with his anxiety about reactions from City Hall.

"Yes. Arrest him. I tell you, he and the wife have connections."

"I did not shoot Charles Larrimer," the doctor said firmly.

"Nevertheless, I think we are going to need to ask you to come back to the precinct with us, Dr. Chapman. You . . ." the officer motioned to some men who came in bearing a stretcher, "get the body. And you two . . . take this man in the wagon with you to the station."

We tried then to convince him that the doctor should not be arrested but they wouldn't listen. Finally Dr. Chapman told us to stop. "Mr. Cabot, take your sister home. I will go with them."

Alden pulled me out of the way as two officers marched the doctor out of the door. They were followed by others carrying the stretcher with Larrimer's body.

Mr. Prendergast was dancing up and down in agitation. "What will Fitz say? What will the mayor say? I must tell them. Oh, what a calamity." He grabbed the policeman yet again. "Keep him in custody. I must tell Fitz. I will tell Fitz. Don't lose him."

The officer frowned at his back as Prendergast hurried away. I could tell he was not happy that the corpse had turned out to be an important man whose death had brought down the scrutiny of City Hall. "You'll have to leave now," he told us. "I have your names. We'll call you if we need you. We're closing down this whole exhibit."

"But where are they taking him?" I demanded to know.

"First precinct." He ushered us out of the shack and out of the grounds of the village.

"We've got to go after them," I said as we watched the wagon pull away through the gathered crowd. Alden put a hand on my arm.

"What good would that do? No, Emily, think. Isn't there someone in the university who can take his part? Someone important?"

Of course, he was right. "President Harper is still in Europe. And Miss Talbot has not returned yet either. Dr. Chapman works with Professor Jamieson, but he's gone to Europe, too. I don't know when he is due back. But the chairman of the doctor's department is in residence. Surely he can speak for him."

"Good. Let's go see him. If he's not the one he'll know who is."

We rushed away and eventually found Mr. Abbott. He was somewhat suspicious and uncooperative but finally agreed to look into the matter. He proclaimed it too late to go into the city that evening but promised to do so first thing in the morning. I was exasperated with worry but my mother firmly backed up Alden's insistence that the only thing we could do was to wait.

EIGHT

We were waiting for Mr. Abbott when he returned to his office in the early afternoon but I was dismayed to see him accompanied by Mr. Lukas. Lukas was a professor in my own department of Sociology, who had opposed my appointment to the fellowship I held, merely on the grounds that I was a woman. He resented that and other actions of mine and was no friend. Dr. Chapman had opposed him in the argument concerning the physical ability of women to do research. He was one of the men whose own history of illnesses the doctor had brought to bear on the argument. Now, he had an air of grim satisfaction as he followed us into Mr. Abbott's office.

"I am sorry to say Dr. Chapman is being held on suspicion of the murder of a Mr. Charles Larrimer and he will most likely be indicted. The newspapers have already gotten hold of the story and the notoriety this brings the university is most unwelcome." Abbott clapped his hat on the desk and turned to confront us. Lukas stood in silence, his arms folded. "In the absence of President Harper I have consulted the university's attorneys. They advise us to distance the university as much as possible."

"But, Mr. Abbott, surely the university will not abandon one of its people to such troubles. You cannot believe Dr. Chapman capable of such a deed? Surely?"

"Miss Cabot, that is not for us to decide. Unfortunately, the past association of the doctor with the dead man's wife has already been discovered by the newspapers and the resulting scandal has put us in an untenable position. All of this has nothing to do with the university and happened before Dr. Chapman joined us." He held up a hand to prevent me from protesting. "I have seen the doctor. He is in good health and asked only that his medical bag be conveyed to him as he wishes to treat some of the inmates. He has accepted a counsel who will be paid by the university to assist with his legal defense. Aside from that, there is nothing we can do in the matter. Dr. Chapman is quite agreeable to this arrangement and I must admonish you, Miss Cabot, to do nothing to increase the notoriety of this incident. It has the potential to do great damage to the reputation of the university and we must do everything we can to prevent that."

I was outraged by this opinion and I argued heatedly that the university should do more to assist Dr. Chapman. Finally I realized that arguing would do no good, especially with Mr. Lukas lurking in the background. I gave up in disgust but I did manage to take on the task of locating and transporting the medical bag to the doctor. Clearly it was assumed that as a woman scholar of the university I must sever any connection to the affair or the doctor.

So it was that late afternoon found me fighting my way through the crowds as I walked down Michigan Boulevard in the heart of the city. I was lugging the worn leather satchel I had obtained from Dr. Chapman's office. The train trip to the city, followed by the walk down the boulevard, was familiar to me. For the past six months I had been making this trip in order to work on the compilation of police statistics. In the course of the project I had made this very trip once or twice a week for several months.

But this day I looked upon my surroundings with a different eye. Compared to the White City of the Columbian Exposition, the real city was dirty, smoky and crowded. The rattles and hoots of the trains over the lake trestles were incessant. The horse-drawn carriages jostled through pedestrians and the cable cars a block away squealed in the background. The great stone buildings had none of the grace of the neoclassical buildings in the Fair. In their height and stark solidity they had more of the grandeur of natural scenery, like great mountains or gorges. I felt, as I had never before, that the city was rather a fearsome place.

I turned into the First Precinct building with some relief. It was a place I knew and where the inhabitants, alien though they might be to me, had become familiar. Indeed, the sergeant behind a high desk and wire cage recognized me at once and nodded towards the stairwell.

"He's in—up in his office, miss." Then he turned back to the men in front of him who seemed to be arguing over something. Remembering that Dr. Chapman was somewhere within the building in the keeping of these policemen, I had a different view of that familiar sight. Never before had I wondered what had brought those other men before the sergeant or what they sought. This time I imagined that, like me, they might be trying to find someone swallowed up in the building. I turned away hurriedly.

That Detective Whitbread should be in this day was beyond what I had dared to hope for. As I made my way up the worn stairs, lugging the medical bag, my spirit lightened. I had dreaded having to explain my mission to jailers but now I would have a guide. It was comforting to know I was headed for the familiar office with the scarred wooden desk in front of the tall window that Detective Whitbread kept open in all seasons. The wooden file cabinets and bookcases were stacked with weighty tomes that Whitbread used to keep himself up to date on the latest theories of criminology. Yet it was his creed that the working detective belonged in the street among the criminals he sought and Detective Whitbread was nothing if he was not completely faithful to the principles he had discovered and adopted for himself. As a result, it was a rare occasion when I had found him in his office during my many trips there. I was glad today would be one of those occasions.

"Miss Cabot, how good it is to see you. But I understood you had completed your work—if not your study, at least your compilation of statistics. Is there more to do?" He stood behind the scarred desk.

"No, Detective Whitbread, it is not about the study. A most terrible thing has happened. Dr. Chapman has been taken for the murder of Mr. Charles Larrimer. It must all be a mistake. He cannot have done such a thing. Won't you help him?"

"Sit down, please, Miss Cabot."

I took the hard wooden chair and looked at him across the desk. A tall man in his forties with thinning hair and a generous moustache, he was one of the most energetic and resolute people I had ever met. We had come to be friends in so far as our very different circumstances allowed it. Today his face was very serious.

"While I have not been assigned to the case, I am aware of the basic facts. It would seem that Mr. Charles Larrimer was found shot through the heart in one of the structures of the Dahomey Village on the Midway. Kneeling over him was Dr. Stephen Chapman. Dr. Chapman claims that, on hearing a shot, he proceeded to the hut and found Mr. Larrimer dead. However, it quickly came to the attention of the investigating officers that Mr. Larrimer was a prominent cotton dealer who had married a woman who was once engaged to Dr. Chapman. They had not seen each other for some years until they met again during festivities at the Exposition. After that meeting they were seen several times alone together. This has led to the theory that Dr. Chapman had found himself once more in love with the woman to whom he had been betrothed.

Since he has provided no reason for being at the Dahomey Village yesterday, when it seems he had spurned the Midway all summer, it is assumed he had arranged to meet the woman's husband. An argument ensued. This fact is born out by some of the natives of the exhibit who, though they can be understood only through an inadequate interpreter, have testified that angry voices were heard coming from the hut. It is believed the argument resulted in tragedy when Mr. Larrimer was shot. The pistol or revolver used has not been located. This is the only fact that in any way contradicts the story and it is thought there may be several ways the doctor could have disposed of the weapon before he was discovered. The search for it proceeds.

"I know this is a shocking story for you to hear, Miss Cabot, but it cannot be denied. Dr. Chapman was found standing over the body without any reasonable explanation for his presence. And since Mr. Larrimer was a very prominent man—apparently being courted by the mayor himself—the authorities are understandably anxious to explain the tragic event and to punish the guilty party in as swift a fashion as possible."

"This cannot be true, Detective Whitbread. He cannot have done this thing." I went on to tell him all I knew of the circumstances except for the tale that Dr. Chapman had told me in confidence that night outside the Music Hall.

Detective Whitbread seemed most interested in my account of Alden's fears for the doctor's safety which was what had prompted us to go hunting for Dr. Chapman. "So, from your brother's story, Dr. Chapman had no previous engagement to meet Mr. Larrimer that evening?"

"No. He was coming to tea with us. It was only when he heard of the warning about something happening at the Midway that he decided not to come."

"This is new information." He sat back as if considering it. "But you have come today to bring the doctor his medical bag?" He rose. "Let me see what I can find out. Do not expect too much. You may have to give it to one of the jailers. Wait here."

He went out the door and I sat forlornly fingering the worn straps of the leather satchel. I had been alarmed by the newspaper stories describing the murder, but I was even more distressed by Detective Whitbread's recital, since I was sure he was privy to the official thinking. I could not believe that it was possible that the doctor had done this thing.

Perhaps ten minutes had passed when Detective Whitbread returned with Dr. Chapman. I stood up in my surprise.

"Wait outside," the detective told a guard who had accompanied them.

Dr. Chapman was in shirtsleeves with the cuffs rolled up and his vest open. He looked weary, as if he had not slept. There was no joy in his greeting—in fact he seemed displeased to see me.

"I brought your medical bag," I said, hoisting it up as my excuse for coming. "Mr. Abbott asked me to bring it." Actually, I had insisted, but I felt that to admit that would have been impolitic. His face relaxed then and he took the bag in his arms. He held it over the desk and looked at the detective. "May I?"

"Certainly."

Dr. Chapman set the bag on the desk and, after moving the few books and papers resting there to the side, he opened the clasp and began to remove the contents. He examined each item methodically, piece by piece, setting each one down on the desk. Throughout the conversation he concentrated on this task.

"How are you?" I asked stupidly.

"As well as may be expected in the circumstances." He did not look at me.

"But what happened yesterday?" I could not help asking. "Why were you there? Alden said you began to come with him but suddenly left. What was going on?"

He paused to scrutinize the label of a bottle of medicine, then set it down carefully. "I had business elsewhere. I regret I was unable to let your mother know before then."

"But why did you go there? Did you go to meet Larrimer? To warn him there would be trouble?"

He did not answer me but suddenly turned to Detective Whitbread instead. "Why did you let her become involved? You know what will come of it. You know this will be a horrible mess. Why don't you keep her out of it?" His tone was bitter.

Detective Whitbread stood up and took a step towards the doctor, looking him in the eye. "Did you shoot Charles Larrimer?"

"No, I did not."

"Did you see someone else shoot Charles Larrimer?"

"No."

"Did you see anyone else there before Miss Cabot and her brother arrived?"

The doctor dropped his stare and turned back to the desk to begin returning his implements and bottles to the bag piece by piece. "I saw no one who could have shot him. In any case, Mr. Abbott has employed a lawyer to handle my case. He will see to my interests in the matter. I will take his advice and not discuss this any further." He completed repacking his bag and snapped it shut. "Now, if there is nothing further, I will bid you good day. Thank you for bringing the bag, Miss Cabot. Time weighs heavily on my hands here and I may as well concern myself with things I know about. I must leave the legal matters to the lawyers."

It was not said unkindly but I felt it as a reproach. He thought I was being officious and only meddling in his affairs. But I could not believe the university community would desert him to face these charges alone. It was not right.

Detective Whitbread opened the door and told the guard to take the doctor back. When he closed it, I realized I might not see the doctor again until he stood accused in a court of law. It was a bit of a shock and I was glad to sink back into the chair.

Detective Whitbread sat at the desk, rearranging the books and papers more to his liking, and then he began fiddling with a dry pen. I waited, anxious to hear his opinion.

"The doctor is most adamant you not involve yourself in his case, Miss Cabot."

"I know, but how can I just stand by and watch him be found guilty of a crime I know in my heart he could never have committed. Is there no hope?"

He considered me. "There are some curious circumstances that have yet to be explained. It seems certain the doctor is protecting someone, but whom? He has engaged himself to take tea with your family, but as he is walking there your brother tells him there will be a disturbance at the Dahomey exhibit—that, by the way, is curious in itself and bears some investigation for there was no disturbance that night aside from the murder of Mr. Larrimer. The doctor rushes off to the very place of danger. He must wish to warn someone whom he has reason to believe will be there. I don't believe it was Mr. Larrimer he was concerned about, do you? He states he arrives, hears the shot and finds Larrimer dead. He will not admit anyone else was there. Whom would he seek to protect?"

"Mrs. Larrimer?"

He looked at me. "Mrs. Larrimer is the grieving widow. I understand she is very much under the protection of the mayor's office. They are angry that this could happen to such an important man. It doesn't look good for the city or for the mayor's plans to keep the Fair open."

"Oh, actually, the mayor was trying to get Mr. Larrimer to influence a cousin of his who is a congressman to get the federal appropriation for that approved." I told him all I had heard on that matter.

"Fitzgibbons. Yes, he is one of the mayor's men. No wonder they are so concerned with the investigation. They'll want a prompt solution."

"So, Dr. Chapman, being the first one on the scene, must take the blame?"

"Viewed without prejudice, Miss Cabot, it must be seen as very suspicious that the man at the scene should be an old lover of the dead man's wife. No, it is not entirely unreasonable to suspect the doctor. But that is not enough. There must be other witnesses." He slapped the desk and stood up restlessly. "And where is the gun? There could not have been much time to dispose of it. Surely someone must have seen something."

"I saw Mr. Weaver loitering outside the exhibit just as we rushed in."

His eyebrows rose. "Weaver. Well, that is an interesting development. It is certainly true that wherever that man goes trouble follows. But he is a slippery character and he covers his tracks."

I looked at him with hope but he shook his head.

"I am not assigned to this case, Miss Cabot. However, I have business on the Midway. I always have business on the Midway these days. It has attracted every scoundrel in the country, including Weaver. And while there I may undertake some quiet investigation of these rumored disturbances that never took place, and perhaps I may interview a few people at the Dahomey Village." He looked at me. "What I may not do is to talk to Mrs. Larrimer. As I mentioned, she is under the care of the mayor's office, probably Fitzgibbons himself. Having failed to protect her husband he will be anxious to spare her any embarrassment."

"I know Mrs. Larrimer slightly. I may be able to see her."

"I cannot advise you to attempt it, Miss Cabot. Dr. Chapman is right, you know. For the sake of your own reputation, you should not be too closely involved in this. It will be a scandal, and if Dr. Chapman is accused of killing a man because he was in love with that man's wife, it will do him no good to have a single young woman seen as championing his cause. We must both be discrete if we do not wish to harm his cause."

I had to protest. "But Dr. Chapman is a friend and as you very well know I owe him much for helping me last spring. How can I stand by and watch him be convicted of such a crime?"

Detective Whitbread patted my arm with a smile. "We will do what we can, Miss Cabot, but discreetly, very discreetly."

NINE

*W*as Dr. Chapman protecting Marguerite Larrimer? He had told me it was an unhappy marriage, but was it unhappy enough to lead the woman to shoot her husband to death? Despite the detective's admonition to be discreet, I determined to visit the Palmer House Hotel before I returned home, in hopes of seeing Mrs. Larrimer for myself. An inquiry at the desk was disappointing. Mrs. Larrimer was not receiving visitors. As I turned away, uncertain of my next step, I found Clara Shea before me.

"Emily. Isn't it awful? Come over here with me."

Clara led me to a corner of the lobby and we sank into comfortable chairs.

"I wanted to express my condolences to Mrs. Larrimer but she is not receiving visitors."

"No, she's locked in her suite with her father and Fitz. They're determined to keep her from the press. But I cannot believe it— Dr. Chapman. Emily, you know he could not do such a thing. You know it. I cannot understand how they could think it."

"It's terrible. But we were there, Clara. Alden and I were there." I proceeded to tell her the whole story and to recount my visit to the police station that afternoon.

"Emily, it must have been Marguerite Larrimer that he went to warn. She must have been there. Listen, when I returned from our ride on the Ferris Wheel yesterday my mother was upset. She and Mrs. Larrimer were supposed to go shopping in the morning but when my mother went for her she wasn't there. She must have forgotten about it completely. Her maid said she had received a note and left. And another thing—when the news came of her husband's death no one could find her then either. They were all over the hotel looking for her. At last, Fitz said she had been lying down with a headache, but I don't believe it. I think she was out and only returned after he came with that slouchy man, Prendergast, to give her the news."

"Perhaps she was at the Dahomey Village?"

"And killed her husband? Perhaps she might, they had terrible arguments sometimes, or at least he would rage at her—or perhaps she didn't kill him but was there and Dr. Chapman told her to go and is protecting her."

"But how could she let him do that? How could she let him be accused of murder like that?"

"I don't know. It's possible she didn't know he would be accused."

"But she must know, now. It was in all the papers."

"She's practically a prisoner up there between her father and Fitz. They've got her barricaded in the hotel suite trying to keep the press from her. My mother tried to invite her to our suite for lunch but they wouldn't allow it. I've got an idea, though. You and your brother were there, you said? Wouldn't it only be right for you to tell her about that yourself? I could say you told me and I thought it was only right to bring you to see her. Yes, that's it. Come on. Let's go up."

She grabbed my hand and took me to the elevator. When we got to the ninth floor the corridor was lined with seedy looking men holding notebooks. I realized they must be newspaper reporters. They attempted to interrogate us but Clara pulled me along, elbowing through them, all the while refusing to answer their shouted questions. When she knocked on the door it opened a crack and I could see a slice of Mr. Prendergast. He murmured to someone inside the room, ignoring the cries of the reporters, and then he pulled us in, opening the door as little as possible and shoving back the pushy men behind us as he closed it again.

There were only a couple of lamps lit and the drapes were drawn. Mrs. Larrimer reclined on a sofa and her father held one wrist as if taking her pulse. Mr. Fitzgibbons sat in a wing back chair at her head. He had his hat in his hand and he played with it nervously. He stood when he saw us while Mr. Prendergast retreated into the shadows. Clara took the floor.

"Mrs. Larrimer. I am so sorry for your loss. But I met Miss Cabot in the lobby and she told me how she was present, yesterday, when your husband was found and I felt sure you would want to know of it. It must be awful for you, not knowing what happened."

"Here, now," said Mr. Fitzgibbons. "I'm not at all sure this is a good idea. The lady is terrible upset as it is."

But Marguerite Larrimer was sitting up, despite the protests of her father. Her white skin glowed against the deep black of her gown. "It's all right, Fitz. Clara is right. I must hear this." She put up a hand to squeeze her forehead.

I was very uncomfortable but I managed to recount my tale, concluding with a description of how Dr. Chapman had been taken away in the police wagon. I wanted to look pointedly at Mr. Prendergast, who had been there, but he was lost in the shadows.

"So, they have arrested Dr. Chapman and accused him of murdering your husband, Mrs. Larrimer, but I do not believe it is true. I am sure it is not."

Mr. Fitzgibbons suddenly stood up and stepped to a side table where he poured himself a drink. I saw there were tears streaming down Mrs. Larrimer's cheeks.

"I know Stephen did not do this thing," she said. "You don't have to convince me."

"You know nothing about it, Marguerite," her father interrupted her. "This is a horrible ordeal but you must allow the police and the courts to handle it. I'm sure you mean well, Miss Cabot, Miss Shea, but Marguerite is distraught. She needs rest and quiet. As her doctor and her father I must demand she be left alone."

"No, Father, it is all right."

"It is not all right. I will have to ask these ladies to leave."

He was quite angry and Clara and I rose, not knowing what else to do. But Mrs. Larrimer rose also and she stepped over to me and took my hand.

"Stephen is the most upright, loyal man I have ever known. He despised Charles, but he would no more hurt him than he would give in to his love for me. Do not believe the lies. There was nothing between us but past sadness."

Her father took her by the shoulders. "Marguerite, listen to me. You must take the draught I have prepared for you and you must go to bed. There is nothing for you to do and it will be a long day tomorrow."

She collapsed in tears on his shoulder and he glowered at us over her golden head.

"Come, ladies," Mr. Fitzgibbons took each of us by an arm. "Let me help you through that rabble outside."

Prendergast opened the door and shut it safely after us while Fitz steered us through the crowd of jackals, trading insults as he went. We got into the elevator and he indicated to the elevator boy that we wished to stop on the fifth floor, insisting that Miss Shea return to her family suite while he escorted me out. But when we reached the lobby he suggested we sit and talk for a minute.

" 'Tis a sorry tragedy, the whole thing, Miss Cabot. We'll not be having Mr. Larrimer's help with keeping the Fair open now but that's hardly the worst of it. To see a woman like Mrs. Larrimer suffer like that and even your Dr. Chapman. He seems a good man. For it to all to come to this is awful. I can't understand it."

He looked confused and tired and I was in complete sympathy with those feelings, so without even thinking I blurted out everything that had happened and what Clara and I had thought. He looked pained. "So, you've a suspicion Mrs. Larrimer was there and the doctor went to warn her. It's an awful thought. But the thing is, Miss Cabot, you'd not be doing your friend Dr. Chapman any good bringing it to light, even if it were so. Think about it. If the reason they're saying he killed the husband was that he was in love with the wife, well, if the woman then came out and tried to say I saw it, he didn't do it, who do you think would believe her? No one. They'd think they were in it together, mark my words. Oh, no, there's nothing that Mrs. Larrimer can do but will harm his cause. No, we've got to look elsewhere."

I realized he was coming to believe that our faith in Dr. Chapman's innocence had merit and I was cheered by that thought, at least.

"It was Mr. Prendergast who told the police about the doctor's past with Mrs. Larrimer. He was trying to get the doctor arrested."

"Prendergast was feared about how the mayor would react is all. He figured City Hall would want swift justice, which they do. It's put a kink in the plans to get his cousin's help with the legislation, no doubt about that." He shook his head. "You say your brother heard there would be a disturbance and he heard this from that Marco and his mate Teddy at the Ferris Wheel. Now, that's a story that could bear some looking into. He's a pretty scoundrel, that Marco. If Larrimer had dealings with him, that's something. And I blame myself for ever introducing him to the man. But, there then, I thought it would amuse him." He scratched his head. "Well, here's a mystery at least I might be able to shed some light on. What do you say, Miss Cabot, shall we go down to the Midway now and confront the rascals?"

I found the idea heartening and quickly agreed. But, as we walked to the train station and Fitz bought us tickets, it occurred to me that the trip was something a lady in my position would not be expected to do. I shook myself. I had no time for such niceties. The truth was that, since I had joined the university, I had frequently found myself in places and with people I would never have talked to, had I remained a ladylike teacher in Boston. I had been surprised at first that the very area of study involving work with the police and criminal statistics was not beyond the boundaries of what was possible for me. It was not. In the name of research, such associations were not only acceptable, they were required. And even opponents of the women students, like Professor Lukas, did not object to the associations required by research. They only insisted that women lacked the physical stamina to pursue them. By the time Fitz had returned and squired me to a seat, I had dismissed my doubts about proprieties as beneath my notice. He entertained me with stories about the mayor and the builders of the Exposition until we arrived and started walking down the Midway.

It was dark, although there were lights along the broad walkway and plenty of lighted signs to entice one into the amusements. The place was both more garish and more mysterious in the nighttime and I was glad to have Fitz's firm arm to cling to. Music and loud laughter issued from some of the tents and theaters, and the huge Ferris Wheel was picked out in electric lightbulbs above us.

When we reached the Wheel, Fitz marched in, boldly saying he'd come to see Marco. That gentleman seemed rather surprised to see us, or perhaps it was surprise at recognizing me on the arm of the Irishman but he was polite to the point of obsequiousness to Fitz and he led us into a ramshackle structure in the corner of the fence. Chasing out a few men who had been playing cards at a rough table in the middle with a single shaded lamp above it, he sat us down on the rickety chairs and brought out a bottle of Irish whiskey and some glasses. I declined with a motion.

"You won't mind if Mr. Fitzgibbons and I indulge, will you, Miss Cabot? I like to remind our friend of the wonders of his homeland left behind. It's Irish whiskey you see, pure as the driven snow."

"And you are full of the blarney, Marco. But that's not what we're here for. It's serious business this." Fitz gulped down the whiskey and couldn't repress a smile. He held out the glass for more while he continued. "You must have heard of the murder by shooting of a Mr. Larrimer yesterday right here on the Midway."

"At the Dahomey exhibit. Yes, of course, I heard."

Fitz took another gulp of whiskey all the time keeping his eye on Marco. "We've reason to believe there was going to be a disturbance at the Dahomey Village and even if Miss Cabot's brother hadn't been warned about it by your chap, Teddy, I'd have said . . . well if anyone would know about a planned disturbance it would have to be my friend Marco. There's not much going on at the Midway that my friend Marco wouldn't know about. Isn't that true?" He glared across the table at Marco who looked solemn but merely poured him another glass of whiskey. "And, furthermore, it seems Miss Cabot herself saw Mr. Larrimer come out of your place of business yesterday afternoon and talk about settling debts. And what was all that about, now, I ask you?"

Marco's face seemed to brighten. He perked up like a dog given a bone to chew on. "Oh, dear, he said that did he?" The dark eyes were turned on me. "I'm afraid you'll be getting me into no end of trouble, Miss Cabot, but there it is." He turned back to Fitz. "Mr. Larrimer did come to see me yesterday, now that you mention it. And it was concerning the purchase of some IOUs that had come into my possession. You know how it is. Someone needs this, someone else needs that, and there's barter to pay for it. Of course, we don't sponsor any games of chance here, you understand. We're much too busy and profitable for that."

Fitz grunted in what I could only imagine was disbelief.

"No, no, but in the course of some other business transactions these IOU's had come into my possession and Mr. Larrimer came to redeem them and I'm glad to say he did redeem them, every one."

"How much?"

"Really, Fitz, you can't expect me . . ."

"How much?"

"Oh, all right, a bit under ten thousand dollars, if you must."

"Ten thousand? Larrimer didn't look like that big a loser."

Marco looked smug. "And, indeed, he was not. For the IOUs were not in his name, you understand. No, he was much too shrewd himself to fall into such an obligation. I could tell that right away, though I only met him a few times. No, the IOUs were incurred by his father-in-law, Dr. Ramsey. It seems the learned medical man occasionally got a little carried away with his gambling."

"But Larrimer put up the dough?"

"Yes, indeed, and I was most grateful, I can tell you, for discreet inquiries revealed the doctor left similar obligations behind him in Baltimore and I was beginning to despair of ever actually seeing the money. So, as you can imagine, Mr. Larrimer made me a very happy man."

Fitz was sipping the whiskey now and glaring at Marco over the rim of his glass. "And this 'disturbance'?" he spat out. Marco looked uncomfortable.

"I know of no disturbance. But you said young Mister Cabot had a dire warning from Teddy." He got up quickly. "Wait just a moment and we'll have it from the horse's mouth, so to speak."

He slipped out the door and Fitz shook his head as if to say, "What to do about such a character?" Then, as if suddenly aware we were alone together, he put down his glass of whiskey and straightened up. Marco returned almost immediately, pushing Teddy before him.

"Evenin' mate . . . miss." He pulled the top hat from his head and held it before him while he looked back and forth between the two of us.

"What's all this about a disturbance on the Midway yesterday, Teddy?" Fitz interrogated him.

"A disturbance, guv'nor? No such thing. Why it was quiet as a church you might say. No disturbance. Just some bloke got himself shot but you couldn't rightly call that a disturbance, you know."

"You told Miss Cabot's brother to take his sister home and avoid the Dahomey Village yesterday. What was all that about?"

He shifted on his feet. "Oh, that, right. Well, that weren't nothing. Some of the lads was thinking of going down and throwin' banana peels at the natives, like." His face beamed. "It weren't no harm meant. I just heard some of 'em talking about it like and I thought it weren't no place for the ladies, so I told Alden, see, so he could take 'em all home." He looked pleased with that.

Fitz stood up and in a few steps he towered over the smaller man. "Well, I'd have to say, for your sake, I'm glad it didn't come off, because, as I thought I made plain before, there will be no disturbances on the Midway. This is our town and if you want the opportunity to stay here and make your profit on this fair you'll behave yourselves. Is that understood?"

There was an ominous silence for a moment, then Marco stepped over and fearlessly clapped Fitz on the shoulder. "All well understood, friend. And no harm done. Now, would you like another glass of whiskey? Or, perhaps you and the lady would like a ride on the Wheel? Yes? Nighttime with all the lights. It's a fantastic sight. You really must see it."

I protested that my mother would be wondering at my long absence and told them I had to return home. Mr. Fitzgibbons looked disappointed but he insisted on walking me back to my lodgings. He was uncharacteristically quiet until we reached my door.

"I don't know if that has helped, Miss Cabot. But Mr. Larrimer was a hard man, a hard man of business. I'm sure there must be other men besides Dr. Chapman who hated his guts. I'm sure if the doctor didn't do it, they'll find who did in the end. Good evening to you."

When I had closed the door I saw again the picture of Dr. Chapman squatting over the body of Charles Larrimer and I shivered. The university was rushing to sever all connection with the doctor. Mrs. Larrimer had not admitted to being there. Mr. Marco and Teddy Hanover denied all knowledge of what had happened. If only Detective Whitbread were in charge of the case I might have some hope that the truth of what happened would be discovered. But he was not. It seemed to me the doctor was being abandoned, a lone figure lost somewhere in the bowels of that large cold building on Michigan Boulevard and I felt cold and numb at the thought. Whatever could I do about it?

TEN

*I*n the morning, I received a note from Clara that she had sent by special messenger. She said her own family and Mrs. Larrimer would all be leaving by train that evening, taking Mr. Larrimer's body back to Sherville, Kentucky, for burial. But Marguerite Larrimer wished to meet with me privately before they departed. If I would come to the Palmer House at one o'clock and ask for Clara, the meeting would be arranged.

Alden insisted on coming along, but I made him wait for me in the lobby. Following the instructions, I found myself in a small sitting room of the hotel, facing the heavily veiled figure of Marguerite Larrimer across a low table with a bowl of chrysanthemums in the middle. Clara delivered me to my seat then quietly left the room.

When the door closed the other woman rolled up the black lace of her veil, so I could view her pale face.

"Thank you for agreeing to meet with me, Miss Cabot. I was not able to speak freely to you in front of my father and Mr. Fitzgibbons. I know that you are trying to help Stephen—Dr. Chapman. I could not leave you to imagine that I would not help your efforts if I could. I wish with all my heart that he could be free and clear from this and it weighs heavily on me that his troubles in this matter have come all on my account. But I am very afraid that what I know and can tell you would only count against him. But you shall judge."

"You were there when it happened, weren't you?"

She rose nervously and walked over to the window, touching the sheer curtain with a gloved hand as if to look out. "Yes. But allow me to explain. My husband . . . but, no, I must explain myself." She sighed. "You know that some years ago Stephen was a student of my father's. We met and fell in love and became engaged. My father did not approve because Stephen was so poor, but when he saw I was determined to have him, my father planned to help Stephen get on in the world. But Stephen was an idealist. He refused my father's help and broke the engagement." She turned towards me. "I know the world believes I dropped him for a richer man, but it is not true. He insisted on releasing me from the engagement. I was heartbroken." She turned back to the window.

"I was devastated to find I meant so little to him. It was really his work which meant so much to him. It was always his work. Then, Charles Larrimer appeared and courted me with lavish presents but, more than that, he made me believe I was the center of his universe, that he could not live without me. Charles always had a completely seductive charm—perhaps you felt it?" She turned to appeal to me, then back to the window.

"It was not until after I married that I found out what he was really like. He was ruthless and single-minded about getting what he wanted. He had learned to be that way in his bitter struggle to redeem his family fortunes after the ruin of the war. He took me to his family home as the crowning decoration. He had spent a fortune restoring it to its earlier grandeur and I, it seemed, was the final piece of the puzzle. But I did not understand that world of the South before the war. I was forever making mistakes and felt confined by my role. He came to despise me and I him. I was miserable." She shivered. "It was an unhappy marriage. But then there was an act of his that proved to me he was capable of inhuman cruelty." She shook her head as if speechless with the memory of some past crime. "I was afraid of him after that." She took a breath and plunged on.

"Before the world, he was a devoted husband to a loving wife. In private, we barely spoke. But when we came here, his cruelest energies were aroused. Perhaps it was meeting Stephen again. Charles knew of our former betrothal. Perhaps it was just seeing all the world that had moved beyond the time he tried to enshrine in his recreation of the world of the South before the war. Beneath the façade of charm, he was a bitter man."

She put a hand across her eyes and squeezed her forehead as if she had a headache. Then she stood a little straighter and continued. "That day he insisted I arrange a meeting with Stephen at the Dahomey Village. I protested. I told him there was nothing between us but he ranted and raged at me and forced me to write to Stephen. I thought the two of us, Stephen and I together, would be able to face him and convince him of the falseness of his suspicions of infidelity."

Her stiff back was to me as she continued to stare out of the window. "But when we got to the exhibit, he began to berate me. He dragged me into that hut off in the corner, screaming at me. When I tried to leave he flung me against a wall. He was mad, mad with jealousy and rage."

She turned then, slowly, to face me. "I saw it had been a mistake to come. He was out of his wits. I managed to escape through a window. I ran away." She spread her hands out. "Don't you see? What would or did happen if Stephen came on him like that? He was like a mad dog. Who could blame him if he shot Charles? And yet who would believe it?" She turned away again. "Mr. Fitzgibbons and my father have convinced me that by telling this story I can only do Stephen harm. Do you think otherwise? Because . . . believe me, Miss Cabot," her forehead was pressed against the pane of the window now, "I would do anything in my power to help Stephen but I fear my intervention could only make matters worse."

I didn't know what to say. She had been there, just as I suspected. And the doctor must be trying to protect her. But why, if they had planned to meet, why had he started to come to tea with Alden? Had something else been planned? Had he suspected Larrimer would harm his wife? Had she really escaped or had she managed to get away and killed her husband in self defense? But he was shot in the back. I couldn't see what might have happened. Without any other testimony, I had to believe what she had just told me. "I suppose since you cannot say you saw another person do the shooting, your story cannot help much. But did you see no other person as you ran away? Was there no one else?"

She turned to look at me, and I saw she had replaced the veil so I could no longer view her face.

"There was no one else," she said dully, and I realized then that she believed Stephen Chapman had murdered her husband. It took my breath away because I had supposed her to be so very close to the man, having loved him and even been betrothed to him. Yet I knew she was very wrong. I just knew it. For a moment I wondered if I should even believe her. But she was very distressed, and, in the end, I thought my doubts uncharitable.

"One more thing, Mrs. Larrimer. That day, at the Midway, your husband discharged some gambling debts. Were you aware of that?"

"What does that have to do with anything?"

"Your husband was shot, Mrs. Larrimer. If Dr. Chapman did not shoot him, who would have? If he had dealings with gamblers then he had dealings with a class of men to whom it would not be strange to settle an argument with a gun."

"I see." Although I could not see her face, I knew she thought I was clutching at straws. "Charles would never incur gambling debts that he did not discharge immediately. He considered it a question of honor." She gave a little laugh, almost hysterical. "I'm afraid it must have been done for my father. He suffers an unfortunate attraction to games of chance. My husband periodically has been required to pay off his debts, a circumstance he was certain to throw in my face. He was not a generous man but he was a proud one. He could not bear for anyone connected to him to have a stain on his honor."

"I suppose your father was grateful for Mr. Larrimer's assistance?"

"Grateful? He, too, has his pride but he has never been ruthless enough to make the sums of money Charles made to pay for indulging his pride. He suffered my husband's merciless rages like the rest of us. And he was obliged to Charles, like the rest of us."

And he must be greatly relieved to have the son-in-law gone and his daughter a wealthy widow, I thought.

"Thank you for telling me all of this, Mrs. Larrimer. I hope that you will communicate your story to Dr. Chapman's attorney so he may judge whether or not it would assist in his defense."

But she was not going to let me off so easily. "I leave it to you, Miss Cabot. I am at your disposal. I must go home to Kentucky to our seat at Sherville to bury my husband. I will return if summoned by you or Stephen or his lawyer. If there is a trial . . ." her voice broke and she stopped, clutching the back of a chair. "If Stephen is put on trial for this I will certainly return but I will do nothing until asked." Then she whispered as she rustled out of the room, "I have done enough damage already." And she was gone.

I sank into one of the sofas, considering what I had heard. So now it was my dilemma. Should she speak, or not? I felt sure Dr.

Chapman would not thank me for my interference. I had come to no conclusions when Clara came back and sat beside me.

"Emily, we will return to Kentucky tonight with Marguerite and her father. I won't be back then until the term starts in a few weeks. But, meanwhile, I did manage to get my mother to tell me something of the mystery in the Larrimers' past. I know none of the details. But she says that Marguerite was assaulted by a Negro. The townspeople became enraged. They seized him and did a public lynching. My mother says . . . poor Marguerite . . . after that her relationship with her husband was never the same."

I stared at Clara. How very odd that in the long history of her life Mrs. Larrimer had just shared with me, this event was never mentioned. She had mentioned an act of inhuman cruelty on the part of her husband. Was it part of this untold story? I left the room unsure what to think about the woman.

In the lobby, I was very much surprised to find Alden in conversation with Dr. Ramsey. The imposing figure of the doctor towered over my brother. The older man wore mourning and both their expressions were solemn as befitted the occasion but I sensed excitement in my brother's animated face.

"Emily, I have been telling Dr. Ramsey how sorry we all are for this tragedy but how we cannot believe Dr. Chapman can have done this awful thing. He tells me Mr. Larrimer was upset about other things during the past few days. Isn't it so, Dr. Ramsey?"

The older man did not appear happy to see me, as if he felt comfortable with a man-to-man discussion of recent events with my brother but was put out at my appearance. Nonetheless, he pulled himself together and responded.

"It is outright slander to suggest there was anything between my poor daughter and Stephen Chapman. That was all over years ago. There was nothing between them and no reason for Stephen to shoot my son-in-law. It is absurd.

"Charles was very upset about a scurrilous pamphlet that was being distributed. It purported to tell the truth about the lynching of Negroes that had happened in the South. Somehow Marguerite had gotten a copy of it and, when he found it, he was furious.

"He insisted on defending the barbarous custom of a mob taking the law into its own hands. It was disgraceful but he defended it. You wouldn't think it from his sophisticated, civilized manners but he was distinctly uncivilized in that opinion. There had been a lynching in his own town, some years ago. I don't know the details. I wasn't there at the time, but it happened. And I heard Charles complain that he had seen a relation of the man who was lynched."

"You mean he saw him here, at the Exposition?" Alden asked.

"So it seemed. It slipped out in a moment of exasperation. He knew my views on the matter and would not want to tell me about it, especially if he were personally involved. We did not always agree on things. Certainly not on this matter."

"But if he had been involved in a lynching and if a relation of the dead man is here," Alden extrapolated, "surely he would be a much better suspect for the murder than Dr. Chapman? Do you know any more about it?"

"No, I'm sorry. As I said, he would not confide in me. Excuse me, here is my daughter. We must depart now."

We said our good-byes and watched as the party, dressed all in black, climbed into coaches that would take them to the train station.

ELEVEN

I had arranged to meet with Detective Whitbread that afternoon at the Dahomey Village and Alden begged to be allowed to accompany me. He was anxious to meet the policeman about whom he had heard so much. I consented more because I knew the detective wanted to question us both than to satisfy my brother's curiosity.

I had not had time to pay much attention to the place on our previous visit. It was in the form of an African village of straw huts that had been moved whole from a country recently vanquished by the French. The huts were unremarkable but the people were completely outlandish. Thin, rangy African Negroes, they wore more beads and feathers than clothing. Presumably the tropical climate of their homeland favored the scant dress but the Midwestern fall weather had begun to bring a chill to the air and the Dahomey natives were hunched over in a vain attempt to warm themselves. They looked miserable.

"I'm afraid the climate is not to their liking," Detective Whitbread remarked. "Too cool. But I understand the Eskimos have a similar problem, only they find our weather too warm. Here, let us leave the poor creatures until an interpreter is available and proceed to the scene of the crime."

We left a group of them in a circle hunched over and rocking back and forth on their bare feet making a sort of keening noise. I felt very sorry for them.

When we reached the hut in the far corner where we had found Mr. Larrimer's body, Detective Whitbread decided to reenact the bloody deed, much to my brother's ghoulish delight. I stood by doubtfully as Alden pointed out where Larrimer had lain with the doctor kneeling over him. Whitbread even had Alden recline on the floor to show the exact angle of the corpse. I shivered at the sight of the dried blood still visible on the dirt floor but it didn't bother Alden. When they agreed upon the exact position, insisting on my opinion, which was given without much enthusiasm, Detective Whitbread carefully helped Alden to a standing position and demanded he stay still. I confess some satisfaction in watching my brother obey this injunction as it was never to his liking to stand still. But we both watched as Detective Whitbread proceeded to back away from Alden in a precise line, extending his arm and keeping it pointed at my brother as he did so.

He ended up in a shadowy corner right beside where I still stood in the doorway, having no taste for the business. Stopping almost beside me, he folded his arms.

"What is it?" asked Alden, nearly jumping up and down in his restlessness.

"The angle of the shot," Whitbread explained. "I examined the body. There were no powder burns on Mr. Larrimer's clothes, which would indicate the shooter was a certain distance away. Unless he was extremely proficient, however, it would not be much further than this, or he might easily have missed his target."

"You think someone might have been standing almost at the door when he was shot?" I asked.

"Possibilities, Miss Cabot, merely possibilities. But what is that?"

He strode forward to the poles and planks that made a side of the hut beyond where Alden stood. My brother could contain himself no longer and followed.

"Oh, one of the planks is broken," he reported, "and pieces of this post have flaked off."

"There are dents, as well," Whitbread pointed out. "It looks like there was a struggle here."

"But if the shooter was back by the door how was there a struggle?" I asked.

"More possibilities, Miss Cabot . . . indications." He disappeared for a moment then returned. "A false wall, actually, forming a small vestibule or, I suppose, a sleeping apartment behind here. There is a small window. The only other outlet from this hut aside from the doorway, I would say. It would be a small man or a woman who would fit through it."

I stepped over to look. This must have been how Marguerite had escaped but I did not feel that I could share her confidences with the detective, not until I had consulted the doctor and his lawyer. The fact that she had been there might only damage the doctor's case.

Detective Whitbread dusted off his hands. "Enough I think for the time being. Now, Mr. Cabot, you are the one, are you not, who was told of a disturbance that was to occur on the Midway that night?"

Alden nodded. "Yes. After we rode the Ferris Wheel, Teddy—Teddy Hanover, one of the barkers—told me. I met him with Mr. Fitzgibbons the night before, he and Marco—the man that he works for." I saw a look of distaste on the detective's face as Alden continued. "He pulled me aside and said there was due to be a bit of a dust up on the Midway up near the Dahomey Village and it would be a good idea for me to get the ladies away and stay away myself. Might be a bit serious is how he put it."

"How well acquainted are you with Mr. Hanover?" Whitbread asked.

"Not well, as I said. But Mr. Fitzgibbons introduced us the night before. I came down here with him after the concert. So I thought he must be all right. Fitz is with the mayor's office, you know."

"I am acquainted with Mr. Fitzgibbons, Mr. Cabot, and while I would not go so far as to malign that particular man, I would caution you concerning those engaged in politics in this city. I regret to say that graft is rampant among our holders of public office and, indeed, is even more certainly to be found among those who hold no office by means of their own efforts but rather only in recognition of their contributions to the election of another. I do not point fingers. I do not accuse. I merely caution you.

"In any case, about Mr. Marco and Mr. Hanover I can be plain," he continued. "They are among the petty thieves and swindlers who have been drawn to the city by the Fair. Beware. They may seem pleasant and accommodating but hold on to your purse. In particular, it is believed they run a gambling den that moves around the Midway to avoid prosecution. It has not yet been proven but I am sure they are behind it."

"At least Alden has little in his purse so he cannot be much of a prospect for them," I told him. "About the gambling—there is some reason to believe Mr. Larrimer had dealings with them over debts. Not his own, but Dr. Ramsey's."

I told them what I had learned on my visit to Marco with Mr. Fitzgibbons. Detective Whitbread frowned. "It is as I suspected. They have sought protection from the politicians. It is graft of the worst sort to betray the public trust in this way but it is my belief that most of the hawkers on the Midway pay some sort of fee to the henchmen of the local political machine in order to operate freely. They refuse to lodge a complaint, however, so it cannot be helped. Beware of Mr. Fitzgibbons. I say no more but do not trust the political man in anything but supporting his candidate. That is the only thing to which he is true."

"This is not a very political circumstance, however," I pointed out. "Mr. Fitzgibbons's interest had been to persuade Mr. Larrimer to help to get the federal funding to keep the Fair open. With Larrimer dead, his interest is gone."

"And Fitz is a good guy," Alden insisted. "He only introduced me to Marco and Teddy to amuse me."

"Very well," said Whitbread. "I have learned there was something afoot that night. Someone paid some rough men to be on hand outside this exhibit. They weren't told what was to happen, only to be ready for a brawl. The odd thing is they were paid but nothing happened. Of course, when the police showed up they dispersed, expecting someone to complain they had taken the money without performing, but, unwilling to risk their skins against a force of the police, they ran away. Contrary to their expectations, they never heard another word about it and were left free to spend their money without complaint. Needless to say, they were very well satisfied, which may explain why none of them care to name their employer, although I have a suspicion your friend Marco was behind it."

"But why would he want a brawl?" Alden asked. "Larrimer had paid up on his father-in-law's debt, hadn't he?"

"So your sister was told, but who is to say if that was true? If Larrimer had refused to pay do you think Marco would admit it after the man was dead?"

"Do you think they could have shot him?" I asked.

"More possibilities, Miss Cabot. Certainly one of the ruffians who surrounded the exhibit that night could have obtained a revolver and done the deed. But I have no reason to believe any one of them did so. Those who have admitted participation swear they were called on only to brawl although that may have been intended as a cover to allow the shooting to take place. Impossible to say."

"How will this help Dr. Chapman?" I asked.

"Patience, Miss Cabot. If we can establish what really happened that night, then we will help Dr. Chapman."

I thought of Marguerite Larrimer's story but I still did not think I could reveal her secret without the permission of those involved. "There is another possibility, something we heard about only this afternoon. I learned that some years ago Mr. Larrimer was instrumental in a lynching and, according to Dr. Ramsey, he saw a relation of the dead man here at the Fair."

Detective Whitbread shook his head sadly. "It is a vile and wicked thing for a mob of men to usurp the duties of the state and take into their own hands the administration of punishment without the due process of law. If Larrimer was involved in one of these lynchings how could we be surprised if revenge fell upon him in the end? It is revenge, not justice, that motivates such acts."

"It was said his wife had been assaulted by the man," I told him.

"What are the exact circumstances? Who was the man? Knowing that, it should be possible to track down any relatives."

"I don't know. I had only the barest details. It would have happened in the town of Sherville, Kentucky some four or five years ago."

"Facts, Miss Cabot, we need facts not rumor. Can you not obtain more information from your source?"

"Clara had it from her mother but most reluctantly. I doubt she could get her to say more, even if she knows it. But she would not have been present. Dr. Ramsey claimed Mr. Larrimer had seen the relative but he has left town and somehow I do not believe he would provide more information since his daughter's reputation is at stake and he, also, was not present."

"Mrs. Larrimer, then?"

I flinched at the thought. Once again I regretted that I could not be frank about my meeting with the widow. But I had promised her to tell only the doctor and his lawyer. I could not admit that, in all she had told me, the lynching had never been mentioned. It seemed to me it was something she intentionally concealed. "I could attempt it, but she has left town and it would have to be done by letter." I thought of how she had not mentioned this incident during our heart-to-heart talk. "I doubt she would cooperate. But I can think of someone who has been collecting information about such occurrences—Miss Ida B. Wells who wrote the section on lynch law in a recent pamphlet. Perhaps she will know of this incident since she has been investigating such things."

"Names and dates are required."

"I will approach her."

"And I will find out what I may about Dr. Ramsey's gambling debts."

"I could try to find out more from Marco and Teddy," Alden suggested. Detective Whitbread was not pleased by this idea and neither was I.

"I strongly advise against any association with those scoundrels," he told my brother, then turned to me. "If there is anything to be discovered about this lynching story, Miss Cabot, the sooner we have the information the better. For the sake of publicity they will hold off the trial of Dr. Chapman for the murder of Charles Larrimer until after the Fair closes. But by that time many of the people who gathered here will scatter and it will be much more difficult to find witnesses once that happens."

I acknowledged this fact and promised to pursue the story as quickly as possible. When we parted outside the gates of the Dahomey Village, Alden and I headed back to the university.

"He is a very upright sort of person, isn't he?" Alden commented.

"That's right. Remember Mr. Fitzgibbons said something of the sort when I mentioned him."

"I don't think they get along, do you? He sounded like he thought Fitz was some kind of crook or something."

"I don't think he meant it like that. The political organizations of the city, especially successful ones like Mayor Harrison's, are well known for doing favors. A very honest policeman like Detective Whitbread would have a hard time trusting them."

"I think it goes both ways."

"What do you mean?"

"Didn't you notice? Fitz's flunky Prendergast was hanging around just outside the gates. I don't know who he was watching, Whitbread or us, but there must be somebody he mistrusts, don't you think?"

TWELVE

*T*he next day I worked at the Liberal Arts Building all morning. Finally, in the afternoon, I found my way to the Haitian pavilion where I approached Miss Wells.

"Good afternoon, Miss Cabot, may I help you with something?" She smiled down at me from her perch on the high stool behind the desk where she greeted people and distributed her pamphlets.

"Thank you, Miss Wells. I have read your pamphlet and am grievously shocked by the descriptions. But it has led me to hope that you might have knowledge that could assist a friend of mine who is in most serious trouble."

She looked surprised. "Certainly, I would assist in any way possible. With the pamphlet we hope to open the eyes of all right-minded people to the great injustice that is taking place with these crimes against our people. But how can I help you?"

"It is a private matter. Is there some place where we could talk?"

With a serious expression on her smooth, dark face, she considered me carefully. Finally, as if coming to a conclusion, she turned away and beckoned to the man who stood behind her. In short order she had established him in her place, retrieved her hat and led me out into the sunshine where we left the grounds of the pavilion to stroll on the graveled walk towards the lakefront.

"I hope you do not mind walking, Miss Cabot. I spend a great deal of time at my desk inside and must take the opportunity to get some air whenever it is possible."

The walk was agreeable to me. Fall was coming on and there was a tangy breeze that cooled the brightly sunlit day. Near the Haitian pavilion there were many colored people among the visitors but as we moved further away, past the exhibits of Germany and Spain and towards the North Pier, the sauntering crowds were mainly white. I saw Miss Wells glance at me several times as if to see whether I would find this problematic but I was much too anxious to gain her cooperation to give it much thought.

I explained to her Dr. Chapman's circumstances and the fact that we had just learned the dead man might have been involved in a lynching some years before. I earnestly entreated her assistance in finding out the facts concerning that matter. But she said she had no personal knowledge of the incident and I was deeply disappointed.

"I had hoped you might have heard of this matter or might know of someone who would have. From your essay, it seemed you have collected evidence of these happenings for some time."

She stopped, then, to lean against a railing overlooking the lake. "It was a lynching in my home town of Memphis that brought these awful matters to my attention in a way that I could not ignore," she told me. "It is when it is a personal experience, Miss Cabot, when you know the good and decent man who is killed and not only that, but whose name is vilified to justify the act. It is when you know the man, and his wife, and are godmother to his little daughter, that you are forced to protest. For lies are invented and propagated to cover the real motives for these acts.

"In that case it was three Negro businessmen who opened a grocery store in a Negro neighborhood in competition with a store operated by a white man. The newspapers spread rumors that colored men were killing white men when, in fact, they were only defending themselves from an assault organized by the white competition. The white men attacked the store and shots were fired. The injured white men had started the trouble by attacking. Nonetheless, the press incited the crowd. Panic and fury flamed up and were encouraged on every side by the white journalists. One hundred colored men were pulled from their houses and jailed. For two nights a colored militia was called upon to defend the jail and to prevent unlawful violence. On the third day, the injured white men were reported to be recovering, the militia was withdrawn and that night the three businessmen were taken from the jail illegally, brought some miles out of town and shot to death. And for this, no one was ever punished.

"It was having personal knowledge of the true circumstances of that act and knowing how it had been misrepresented in order to justify the unjustifiable, illegal act of the lynch mob that caused me to feel outraged, Miss Cabot. It is since that time that I have sought to investigate the facts of the circumstances surrounding these acts of violence against our people. For the true nature of these acts is covered by lies and rumors. It is only by exposing the facts of the situation, and the racial prejudice that is the true cause of this unlawful violence, that we can hope to persuade people like yourself of the evil that is happening and the need to put a stop to it."

"Everyone who reads your pamphlet must be very shocked," I told her. "I think you must succeed in persuading everyone."

"But it is not that easy," she told me. "Even in the North they do not wish to hear. They do not want to be persuaded. In fact, I have found I must travel to England where the anti-slavery sentiment first began, to find people willing to be persuaded. I spent most of last year in England where, at last, I found people willing to listen and willing to protest."

"But you continue to document these terrible lynchings?"

"Yes. There are some papers willing to investigate. We keep files and have even sent investigators to find the truth sometimes.

The pamphlet is only the first to document this injustice. We hope to publish more."

"In the records you keep, might there be some mention of this lynching in Sherville, Kentucky?"

She stood back from the railing and turned a troubled gaze to my face. "I do not know. It is possible. But, as I have said, we have found frequently that the facts of the matter, the true causes in particular, may be purposely misrepresented."

"I do understand, Miss Wells. I do not seek to excuse any past lynching or other actions of the dead man, Mr. Larrimer. But if that act in the past contributed in any way to the man's violent death, we need to know in order to prevent an injustice from happening to my friend. Surely you can understand that, having seen *your* friend suffer so unfairly."

She stood up straight, gathering all of her small height, which was barely over five feet. "Very well then, Miss Cabot. Come with me."

I hurried to keep up with her as she marched directly back to the Haitian pavilion. Once determined in a course of action Miss Wells was not to be interfered with. Ignoring greetings from those we passed, she led me back to her desk where the tall, prosperous looking man still held her place.

"Miss Cabot, this is Mr. Barnett, who is one of the owners of the newspaper the *Conservator*."

Mr. Barnett stepped down and nodded warily.

"Mr. Barnett, Miss Cabot is seeking information concerning a lynching that supposedly happened in Sherville, Kentucky several years ago. She has asked whether she may see the files we keep on such happenings." She turned to me. "Mr. Barnett has allowed us space in the office of his newspaper—which is in the basement of his house—for storing these files."

Mr. Barnett was regarding Miss Wells with skepticism but I could see that he was used to giving in to her when she was determined. "I don't believe anyone is at the office today but I will return there shortly. If you come later this afternoon you should be able to see the files. However, I think it best that you personally escort Miss Cabot and assist her in her quest."

I saw them exchange a glance. Miss Wells looked as if she might have objected but seeing something in his eyes that was just as firm as her own determination, she appeared to give in.

"Very well. If you will return at five o'clock, Miss Cabot, we can take the train to visit the office."

"I will return then. I am very grateful to both of you for any assistance you can give in this matter," I told them with great relief. They both turned towards me as if they had momentarily forgotten my presence. I dropped a slight curtsy and hurried away before either of them could have a change of heart.

When I returned at five o'clock, Miss Wells and I took the elevated train towards downtown, getting off at 31st Street. We walked through a prosperous Negro neighborhood of brick row houses, until we reached a particularly fine looking house surrounded by iron grillwork. Miss Wells led me through the yard and around the side to the back of the house.

"There is a separate entrance for the paper," she explained as we reached the rear but then she stopped dead, so I nearly collided with her.

"What is it?"

But that was obvious when we moved forward again. Someone had broken a glass window and the door hung open.

"Shall I go for help?" I asked but she waved me back and I was amazed to see her reach into her bag and pull out a revolver.

"Hello, Mr. Barnett. Are you there?" Fearlessly she stood in the doorway, leaning forward to shout. But I realized she had the revolver balanced against the wood of the doorframe and she stood on tiptoe ready to flee at the first sign of danger. Then, I saw her drop down on her heels and hurry inside, letting the gun drop to her side. Peering through behind her I could make out Mr. Barnett at the end of the hallway, holding a bloody handkerchief to his head.

"You are hurt, come." Miss Wells ushered him back into the far room, which proved to be the kitchen and, sitting him down at the table, she carefully put the gun down and began to examine the wound on his head. He motioned feebly as if to wave her away but soon gave in to her ministrations. She quickly gathered water, towels and bandages and began to clean and bind the wound.

"It was a burglar. I don't know what he took. Not much. He didn't go upstairs but he knocked me out and was gone when I woke up. Lucky Mrs. Spender wasn't here."

Ida Wells glanced at me over his head. "Mrs. Spender is the housekeeper. Mr. Barnett is a widower with two children. It is a very good thing they were not here. Stay still now." As she worked on his head she noticed that I was staring at the gun on the table. "Yes. I have carried that since my newspaper office in Memphis was ransacked and they threatened to strip and beat me if I returned to that city," she told me grimly. "I have not returned, but neither do I intend to let anyone offer me violence without attempting to defend myself."

She worked on him some more and they decided not to summon the police until Mr. Barnett verified what was missing. When he checked the living spaces, he found that nothing was gone. He appeared to be satisfied that the burglar must have been scared away before he could make off with anything of value. They were very reluctant to consult the police, as they had little trust in those representatives of the justice system.

Finally, Miss Wells led me to the cluttered apartment near the back door that was used as the newspaper office. Here some of the papers were strewn about, and there was some conjecture that the break-in had been an act of vandalism against the paper, but nothing was really damaged. It was only when we went to search for the lynching files that it seemed obvious some were missing. They were kept in a series of folders arranged by date and place but after searching for more than an hour we found no records for a lynching in Sherville. By then, Ida and Mr. Barnett had come to the conclusion that some of the files were missing, although whether they had disappeared that afternoon or any time in the previous month they could not say for sure.

I was greatly disappointed but we had to give up and I sat back on the hard wooden desk chair, clearly discouraged. Miss Wells took a big breath. "In that case, the only thing to do is to send an investigator."

I saw Mr. Barnett frown. He was resting on a worn couch in a corner of the room. Ida saw his expression but shook her head resolutely. "No, it is the only thing to do. Frequently the records are misleading in any case and it is necessary to send someone to interview people who were there."

"You know that is very expensive and sometimes the results are equally unreliable." Mr. Barnett looked stormy.

"It is true. We have to be careful." She turned to me. "Usually, it is necessary to employ a white investigator. The white people involved would never talk to a colored man. On the other hand, it is necessary to provide introductions to the Negro community for him, otherwise he will never get any cooperation there. And the choice of investigator is very important. It must be someone with experience and integrity. We have had one man charge us for the trip and then do no more than repeat the lies and rumors that were spread by the white newspapers at the time. But we have had good results with other investigators."

I could see Mr. Barnett was unenthusiastic about this suggestion, but Ida was insistent.

"I am afraid it may not be possible, in any case," I told her. "The doctor is not wealthy. I doubt he could afford the expense.

I can consult with him and his lawyer, I suppose, but I doubt it will be possible." I couldn't help remembering the dread I had felt when I saw Dr. Chapman and the premonition that I would not see him again. The fate hanging over him seemed very heavy and I had no confidence that he would be found innocent despite my conviction that he did not shoot Mr. Larrimer.

"There is a fund," Ida began.

"No, Ida," Mr. Barnett protested.

"Yes," she said firmly. "The purpose of the fund is to help to document lynchings. This was a lynching."

"We haven't even seen anything to prove that. There were no records," he pointed out.

She glared at him. "Miss Cabot has heard testimony, even though it is secondhand. Do you think anyone would claim a lynching had occurred if it had not?" she demanded.

Mr. Barnett hung his head and Ida turned back to me.

"There is a fund. We will need to advertise for an investigator and to interview, in order to find an honest, trustworthy man. When will the doctor be tried for this?"

"Some time after the Fair closes—probably soon after."

"Then we must hurry. These things take time." She began to write on a piece of paper. "I will compose the advertisement and have it sent out tomorrow."

"I am so very grateful," I said. I realized that the purpose of the fund was to vindicate Negro men and women who had been the victims of lynch law. I knew Mr. Barnett objected to this use of the funds to help with the investigation of the death of a white man who may very well have been responsible for a lynching. "Perhaps my mother and I may solicit contributions from others to try to replenish these funds," I suggested.

"That would be very welcome," Miss Wells told me. She glanced at Mr. Barnett. "But it is not required. The purpose of the fund is to document the truth about as many of these incidents as possible. It is only by finding out the truth and making it public that we can gather enough public opinion against the evils of lynch law and bring the practice to an end. If you will come to me at the pavilion in a few days I will let you know our progress."

Mr. Barnett insisted on accompanying us when we departed. We tried to persuade him he should rest and recover from his wound but he said it was slight and he needed the exercise. We headed for the elevated train station and said goodbye to Miss Wells at the house of the local minister where she was staying. Mr. Barnett continued with me the remaining distance. He was very quiet.

"I am extremely grateful for the assistance you and Miss Wells are providing," I said.

"Miss Wells is an extraordinary person," he replied. "She is passionate in pursuit of justice. She will be heard whatever the price."

"She is a most extraordinary person," I agreed. "She reminds me of the fairy tale about the emperor's new clothes," I commented and, when he gave me a quizzical look, I hurried on. "It's the story about an emperor who gets tricked by a magician into thinking he has on a magnificent set of clothes when really he is wearing nothing. But everyone else is so afraid of him they don't dare to say anything and instead agree with him when he insists that they admire his magnificence. Everyone goes along and pretends they see his clothing, praising him all the time, until one innocent and honest child points out he has on no clothes at all."

Mr. Barnett chuckled. "I think you have something, Miss Cabot. I do believe you have captured Miss Wells's character faithfully. In that case she would be sure to tell the man, king or no king, that he should be ashamed of himself and he'd better go right home and get dressed." He laughed.

We reached the elevated train station, which was at the end of the block.

"You should be safe enough from here. Good night, Miss Cabot."

I surprised him by extending my hand but he shook it cordially enough. Then he turned away and began to walk home, still chuckling to himself over the fairy tale.

Although I still could not see a good end to the situation, it was with a considerably lighter heart that I returned to our lodgings that night and told my mother and brother all that had occurred.

THIRTEEN

*T*he next afternoon I traveled into the city to meet Detective Whitbread at his office. I thought he would be pleased at the plan to discover facts concerning the Sherville lynching and I hoped he might even be able to recommend an investigator. I barely noticed the crowds in the street as I hurried along, hoping all the while that he might have discovered some clue to the mystery already.

There was an air of tension in the precinct when I arrived and the desk sergeant treated me with unusual formality when I told him I had an appointment with Detective Whitbread. I did not know what to think of the reluctance in his manner when he finally allowed me to ascend the familiar staircase.

Reaching the top, I found myself face to face with Mr. Fitzgibbons.

"Miss Cabot." He seemed as surprised as I was. "Whatever are you doing here?"

"I have an appointment with Detective Whitbread. As I mentioned to you, I have been consulting with him concerning a study we are doing at the university." Since the detective's assistance with the doctor's case was unofficial and he had advised discretion, I did not admit the true object of my visit to Mr. Fitzgibbons.

He flushed and glanced back at the office door. He seemed confused. "He's in. For the moment, at least. These are difficult days in the city, Miss Cabot. Sometimes we are called upon to do difficult things. But you must excuse me."

With that he clattered down the stairs leaving me mystified but when I got to the office door I could see that something was amiss. There were packing crates stacked around the room and Detective Whitbread was energetically removing volumes from the shelves. He straightened when he saw me.

"Miss Cabot. I hoped I would see you before I left. I was afraid I would miss you."

"You are leaving?" It was a blow. I realized, then, how much I had been depending on his help and advice during this crisis.

"I am afraid so. I have been transferred to an outlying district. Without cause, Miss Cabot, I assure you. Without cause and I will lodge a complaint with the Board of Commissioners. There has never been any stain or blot on my record and I defy them all to attempt to besmirch my reputation. I will fight this to the end."

"How terrible. Have you been accused of some wrongdoing?"

"Not openly. They wouldn't dare. I have no doubt it is the result of the great god of graft, Miss Cabot. It afflicts our politicians and poisons our system. It is the enemy of us all. We must fight it."

I had never seen the detective angry. He was not a man to give way to his emotions. He valued logic and a scientific approach above all but I could tell that he was sorely tried by the present situation.

"I am sure they are very wrong to use you in this way." I remembered the guilty look on the face of Mr. Fitzgibbons. So this was what he meant. I hesitated to mention his name. "But why would they do such a thing?"

He turned back to packing more books. "I have no doubt that in pursuit of my lawful duties I have, so to speak, stepped on the toes of someone with influence. I have a great suspicion it may be due to my efforts to shut down an illegal gambling operation on the Midway. But I will lodge a complaint and they will be unable to justify this action, I assure you."

"But meanwhile you are transferred?" I sank down into the chair in front of the desk.

"Officially. I have a considerable amount of leave owed me, however, and I may find it convenient to take some of it while my complaint goes forward." He looked across and must have noticed my expression. "But do not worry, Miss Cabot. I will be sure to prevail. I may request a letter from you and Mr. Reed describing my assistance with your study."

"Assuredly, Detective. Mr. Reed and I will be anxious to assist you in any way we can. I will contact him and ask him to draft a letter as soon as I return to the university."

"That would be most helpful. Allow me to give you an address where it may be sent."

He sat down at the desk, opened an ink bottle and transcribed the information. As he handed it to me I realized he was taking the situation very calmly but I myself felt shaken.

"Do not worry, Miss Cabot. I assure you it is merely a temporary set back. A vexing one, it is true, but there are many influential people that I have assisted over the course of my career and it is at times like these that they can and will attest to my abilities and integrity. One cannot give in to this kind of pressure. You can believe me when I tell you that there is no one in this city who would dare to impugn my integrity."

"I am very sure you are right."

"I know you worry about Dr. Chapman. I confess, it concerns me that I may be prevented from continuing that investigation. I have been warned off the Midway, which is why I suspect I was getting close to finding the gambling den. What I discovered was that Dr. Ramsey lost a considerable amount of money and was unable to pay his debts. Furthermore he did not approach his son-in-law to repay the money but, rather, attempted to hide it from that gentleman. When Larrimer was approached by those who held the doctor's IOUs he was furious with his father-in-law. How he might have sought to punish the man, I do not know, but apparently he was heard to threaten those who ran the gambling den with exposure. According to your account Marco claims he paid up in the end but we have only his word and I would not trust that villain for a minute. If he actually refused to pay, and threatened exposure instead, they would have every reason to attempt to silence him."

"Oh, but surely that must help the doctor's case." I was excited by this news but he shook his head.

"Not without proof, Miss Cabot. My sources are all third hand and Marco will swear the debts are paid. Indeed, unless the gambling ring is exposed he can deny knowledge of the existence of debts. It is not very hopeful."

"But there must be some way to prove it. How can they believe Dr. Chapman would kill him when he had dealings with such men?"

"It is very difficult to prove. But did you have any success finding out about the lynching?"

I told him all that had passed in my dealings with Miss Wells and Mr. Barnett.

"It is unfortunate that there were no records. I find it highly suspicious that Mr. Barnett's property was broken into. It is vital to find out the facts of that case. If there is any truth in the assertion of Dr. Ramsey that a relative of the lynched man had been in touch with Mr. Larrimer, it is essential to find out the particulars so this person or persons may be interviewed and their actions at the time of the murder investigated. How soon can they dispatch a detective?"

"Miss Wells is placing an advertisement but they say it is necessary to be careful of the choice. I was hoping you might be able to recommend someone who could be trusted."

"Yes, I can see that an unreliable man could easily take down the first tale he was told and fail to do a thorough investigation. It is Sherville, Kentucky, you say? The job might take a week, possibly more. Time is of the essence. They will schedule the trial immediately after the Fair closes and I am sure they will push to make it as short as possible. I very much fear the doctor may be a victim of the desire to clean this up as soon, and as quickly, as possible."

He pondered silently.

"Can you suggest someone? Is there anything I can do to find someone suitable? Can you offer any advice?" I pleaded.

He looked up as if coming out of a dream. "Hmm. Yes. Well, I think the best plan will be for me to go. Yes, I was planning to take leave in any case. Yes."

"But your own complaint. Will this not interfere with your proceedings?"

"It could delay them. But I can prepare the basic submission and begin the process before departing."

"Are you sure this would not hinder you?"

"Miss Cabot, you must understand that if your friend Dr. Chapman is found guilty, he will surely hang. His case is much more pressing than my transfer. I must tell you that even if Mr. Larrimer were shot by the gamblers I see little hope of finding evidence in time. And if I remain, this present action against me will prevent me from pursuing that line since I am barred from going to the Midway. Investigation of this lynching matter, even if it does not lead to the killer, may at least allow Dr. Chapman's lawyer to prove that Mr. Larrimer's character was such that there were others in this world who might have reason to kill him."

This speech thoroughly frightened me, so I stood up, prepared to agree to the plan and anxious to start.

It was typical of Detective Whitbread that with my help he was able to complete his preparations within the hour and return with me to the Fair where we sought out Miss Wells immediately. I was afraid he would be offended when, despite my recommendation, she insisted on questioning him closely on how he proposed to approach the task. But I found, on the contrary, he appeared to approve of her attention to detail and he described the proposed investigation in detail exhaustive enough to satisfy even Miss Wells as Mr. Barnett and I looked on in wonder at the tenacity of both of them. The terms were discussed and agreed upon in equal detail and Detective Whitbread insisted she prepare several letters of introduction to members of the Negro community then and there, before he departed.

When all was settled, we parted with a promise of frequent written reports and I left with the impression that even the skeptical Mr. Barnett was satisfied that, if the truth of the Sherville incident could be uncovered, Detective Whitbread would be the man to do it. But I was left with nothing to do and I was only too aware that the Fair was scheduled to close at the end of October, and thus the trial of Dr. Chapman was inevitably approaching. I knew I could believe Detective Whitbread when he said the doctor would hang if some other evidence could not be found.

FOURTEEN

I had great confidence in Detective Whitbread, so I began the following week with some hope, but it proved too weak to sustain me for long. Time was moving on and the last days of the Fair were getting closer, yet no one seemed able to do anything to clear our friend, the doctor. I had finally managed to arrange an appointment with Mr. Leventhal, the lawyer who had been engaged for Dr. Chapman. Arriving at his office in plenty of time, I was made to wait an hour before he would see me. Sitting in the outer office, while all the people coming and going were male, I was made conscious of the perceived impropriety of my visit. It made me long for my father's presence. Had he been alive he would have had no difficulty in interceding for Dr. Chapman. He would have known the people to consult and they would have been impressed by his knowledge and reputation. I knew in my heart he would have been successful where I was floundering in my efforts to assist the doctor. The world of lawyers and judges was a world of men. They would find any attempt at interference on my part to be incomprehensible. Yet Alden would be no better received and I could not trust his careless manner. Besides, I could not share Mrs. Larrimer's secret with anyone but the doctor and his attorney.

When I was finally admitted to the inner office I found Mr. Leventhal to be a stout man in late middle age who greeted me coldly and regarded me with disapproval. Nonetheless, I proceeded to relate to him all that Marguerite Larrimer had told me. He was not pleased by the story.

"Of course, I will consult with my client, Miss Cabot, but I cannot imagine that this story of Mrs. Larrimer's could do anything but damage the doctor's case and I will advise him against attempting to pursue it.

"I must also counsel you, if you wish to be of assistance to Dr. Chapman, you would be well advised to cease interference in his affairs. He is accused of a most serious crime and it cannot help either his reputation or your own for you to be linked to him in any way." He made an expression of distaste and I perceived to my humiliation that he believed me the victim of some misguided infatuation with the doctor.

"All of the doctor's friends must be concerned with his welfare and unable to believe he could have done the deed he is accused of," I told him, but my conviction wavered as to the rightness of my own actions. "Dr. Chapman saved my life when I was ill last year, and, perhaps of more importance to me, he defended my academic reputation while I was ill. I might have lost my fellowship altogether if it weren't for him. Of course, I feel anxious at his jeopardy now."

Another moue of distaste crossed the lawyer's features. "It is another circumstance that can be of little use in defending my client from the accusations he faces." He stood up to signal an end to the interview. "Thank you for coming to me with the information, Miss Cabot. I will, as I said, consult with my client but I must ask you, in the meantime—if you wish to help Dr. Chapman—do not relate this story to anyone else." He glared at me.

"Of course. I have told no one, nor will I."

"Very good. Good day then, Miss Cabot." He opened the door and shooed me out.

I had fulfilled my promise to Marguerite Larrimer but I knew neither the doctor nor his lawyer would thank me for my efforts and indeed, I received a curt note from Mr. Leventhal within a few days that dismissed the story as damaging and warned me again to hold my tongue about it.

Preparations were underway for the start of the fall quarter at the university. But I found it difficult to rekindle my enthusiasm of the year before. I remembered with regret the early days at the Hotel Beatrice where we had first met Dr. Chapman and he had helped us by providing empty beer bottles to serve as makeshift candlesticks for the dining room. In those happier times I never could have imagined that a year later would find the doctor arrested and accused of a scandalous murder. I was frustrated by my inability to do anything about what I considered the imminent act of serious injustice that would put Dr. Chapman on trial for his life. How could I go back to my study of sociology and criminal statistics without being able to do anything to right such an obvious wrong? The city merely wanted a scapegoat and they were willing to use the doctor. It angered me.

When Dean Marion Talbot returned to open and prepare the new women's dormitories, for which construction had only just been completed, she interrupted her work to hear the whole story as it poured from my lips. She shared my alarm and rushed off to consult with President Harper and others. But when she called me to her office to tell me what she had found out, I was disappointed. In the end her advice was galling.

"Dr. Chapman is in great jeopardy," she told me with a grim expression. "We are all doing as much as we may to help his case. The university has arranged to fund his defense and we have offered to provide testimonials from many of his colleagues and professors concerning his character and integrity. His lawyer must decide who can best help his case. But there is also virtue in what we must refrain from doing in order not to damage his case,

Emily. Because of the accusations of scandal involving his past association with Mrs. Larrimer, it is particularly important that we not give any excuse for the prosecution or the press to insinuate any lapse of propriety or inappropriate behavior on his part during his tenure here. Indeed, as we all know, there is none to be found, but we must guard against any such accusations being invented. As a result, it must be President Harper and the men of Dr. Chapman's department who speak for him. And it must be done in a reasoned and measured manner in order to counter and make ridiculous these claims that he is in any way capable of scandalous behavior.

"So, Emily, I am afraid it falls to you and me, and the other university women who know and value Dr. Chapman, to help him by doing as little as possible. It is only too apt to give rise to scurrilous rumor and damaging speculation if we attempt to publicly defend or support him now. Because of the nature of the accusations against him, we are forced to leave it to our male colleagues to take up his defense publicly."

Of course, I knew she was right but it worried me. "Men of the university, including Mr. Lukas, I suppose. He bears a grudge for what happened in the spring."

"I am afraid you are right. Mr. Lukas is a formidable enemy in the circumstances and he will take every advantage of the situation. But that is all the more reason for you to be discrete, my dear. Sometimes the most difficult task must be to have the discipline to await developments, Emily. But if this is the only method to aid our friend, we must have the strength to bite our tongues and be patient."

I did not tell her of the investigations of Detective Whitbread already underway, reasoning, perhaps speciously, that he was employed by Miss Wells and Mr. Barnett, not me. But I felt the burden heavy if my task was to sit still and do nothing as the time passed away, drawing ever closer to the trial and the uncertain doom beyond it. And it was a bitter thought to realize that, if Clara and I had not been so anxious to get Dr. Chapman out of his laboratory and into the Music Hall in September, he might never have met with Marguerite Larrimer and certainly none of this would have happened. I remembered with self-disdain how we were so sure we knew better than the doctor what would benefit him then. It was a very bitter thought.

Dean Talbot again offered me the position as her assistant in one of the new dormitories, Nancy Foster Hall, of which she was head. At any other time I would have relished the opportunity to participate in the final arrangements and decoration of the new building so generously donated by a Chicago woman. But I could not concentrate on planning festivities and I dreaded the departure of my mother and brother, who at least shared my anxiety about the doctor's fate. I only realized how deep that dread was when my mother announced she had decided to stay on for another month.

"I found an economical apartment," she told me. "It seems with the Fair closing there are a number of very good bargains available for apartments that will be left empty when the visitors leave."

I was amazed at the relief I felt and we decided I would share the rooms to save the money for board that quarter. No definite date was set for my mother's departure.

"And Alden will be glad to stay longer," she said. I was less satisfied than my mother by this inducement. I thought my brother spent too much time as it was on the Midway, and I feared he would succumb to the influence of bad company, but my mother was sanguine.

"There are many exciting new inventions at the Fair. I cannot help but think your brother's interest in them is healthy. Who knows what it may lead to."

I could imagine all sorts of negative results but I held my tongue, deeply grateful to have my mother continue by my side at this difficult time.

My professor, Mr. Reed, returned and we composed letters of reference praising Detective Whitbread and sent them off. But we found that without that gentleman's support we could get no more cooperation from the city in pursuing our research. Requests for contacts and assistance were ignored or refused and we were hard put to move to the next level of investigation without them. With my original research at this impasse, I found the other courses of study I had selected with so much enthusiasm in the spring, now seemed irrelevant and devoid of interest. I think if it had not been for my mother's pride and her conviction that my father would have wanted me to continue my studies, I might have given up entirely that fall. That is how low my spirits had fallen.

I visited the Haitian pavilion almost every other day in hopes of a report from Detective Whitbread. He had made it clear that since he was employed by Miss Wells, his reports would all be addressed to her. Sometimes I brought contributions which my mother had raised for Miss Wells's campaign but often it was only to inquire for news. The first report was not encouraging.

Dear Miss Wells,

(I trust you will share this with Miss Cabot whom I know to be materially interested in this investigation. However, I leave that to your discretion as being the proper addressee of this report as my employer.)

I arrived Monday. After establishing myself in rooms let by a Mrs. Wilcombe (address provided below), I first visited the local sheriff's office to ascertain the existence of any records of the case.

At first Sheriff Butler refused to admit any such unlawful seizure of a prisoner had taken place. I found it necessary to visit the office of the local newspaper where, for a gratuity (listed in the attached memorandum of expenses), I was allowed to peruse past issues of the publication. While such perusal is customarily provided without charge, I think you will find the small amount given over was a good investment when I tell you that it succeeded in loosening the tongue of the attendant clerk who did, in fact, remember the incident and its approximate date, thereby saving me a considerable amount of time in locating the relevant reports. Transcriptions of the most pertinent stories are attached.

In brief, on September 24, 1886, Mr. Charles Larrimer brought a complaint against a William Jones, eighteen, of Sherville, alleging he had assaulted Marguerite Larrimer, wife of the complainant, beating and raping her. Mr. Larrimer had discovered the young Negro, who was employed as a field hand on his estate, in the act and, with the help of his foreman and several other men employed by Mr. Larrimer, subdued Jones and brought him to the sheriff's office where he was incarcerated to await the next county court proceedings.

On the following morning the newspaper ran an editorial deploring the crime and warning of the need to make an example of the miscreant based on the fear that the crime would be repeated and become commonplace if it was not dealt with swiftly and severely. The nature of the editorial was extremely inflammatory. While not openly advocating a lynching, the writer used examples of similar crimes in other towns that had resulted in such vigilante acts and suggested Sherville would find itself disgraced by comparison.

Apparently that evening a mob of fifty white men entered the jail and removed the prisoner. (The newspaper accounts are silent on where the sheriff and his deputies were when this act of lawlessness was perpetrated, nor do they recount any resistance on the part of these officials.) Jones was taken by wagon to a large tree on the outskirts of the town where more people had gathered including women and children (all white, of course). There Jones was hung, shot and the body mutilated and finally burned. (I will leave the newspaper account to provide the gruesome details of this disgraceful act.)

I could find no newspaper account of any prosecution of the vigilantes who perpetrated this violence. The only other mention of the incident is the editorial (also transcribed below) from the following week, where some effort is made to defend this taking of the law into the hands of the mob, although it is written in general terms without detail as to the persons involved.

Armed with this testimony of a crime, I returned to the sheriff's office where, finally and only after I had pointed out the number of statutes broken by the described acts and the prescribed sentences for such offenses, the sheriff did admit to knowledge of the incident. He claimed there was a single deputy on duty on the night in question and said the man had been overpowered and immobilized by the mob. When I asked about subsequent investigations of the incident, he became evasive but finally admitted that virtually every white male in the town had been involved. "What could I do? Lock them all up?" I pointed out that such an occurrence would be considered a conspiracy and that normal investigative procedures would lead to identification of the instigators. Of this he refused any knowledge and, when I pressed him on the involvement of Charles Larrimer in the deed, he appeared to become frightened and claimed the man who was the supposed injured party—in that his wife was the one assaulted—was not even present at the lynching.

(If I may suggest I believe an official complaint should be lodged with the state district attorney against this sheriff citing negligence on his part. While the fact that this happened some five years ago may result in little in the way of action, it will remain on the official record. At times this can be used to prevent a recurrence of this type of offense.)

Having gotten as much as I could from this most uncooperative official, I proceeded to the Larrimer estate where I requested an interview with Mrs. Larrimer. This was vehemently denied by her father, Dr. Ramsey. I did interview that gentleman but found him singularly unhelpful. He claims he was not present in Sherville at the time and that he knew nothing of the incident. He said his daughter was under doctor's orders not to be disturbed (presumably he is her doctor) and he pointed out that even if she weren't she was under no obligation to submit to questioning by a private individual (which is correct). He protested what he called this effort to malign Charles Larrimer, who is now dead. I then attempted to question him concerning his own gambling debts but he became angry and demanded I leave.

I next approached Olivia Nokes and Thomas Smith, servants of the Larrimers and members of the local Negro Baptist church where I had taken the letters of introduction from Miss Wells. They were extremely reluctant to submit to questioning. In the circumstances, where an act of violence is allowed to go unpunished without even an attempt at investigation, such reluctance is to be expected. People still living under the threat of such violence will tend to refuse to cooperate for fear of reprisals.

As a result I must wait until Sunday services at which time I hope to enlist the aid of Reverend Parsons, the local pastor, to help me convince them to relate the story behind the lynching. I believe I have succeeded in convincing the Reverend that such cooperation is necessary, but I will have to wait on the result, as only he can convince the members of his congregation of their duty and obligation to provide testimony concerning the alleged crime. I will report on the results of this interrogation as soon as possible.

Yours truly,
Henry Whitbread

FIFTEEN

While I was grateful to have my mother continue with me, I found I missed the companionship and camaraderie that had made my first year at the university so happy. I especially missed Clara, who had become my best friend, and I regretted the currents that had arisen during her visit to the Fair, which had caused us to drift apart. I knew she felt it, too, when we met one day by chance and we both began to pour out our news. It was a happy recognition that our friendship still existed but since we both had classes to attend we decided on the spot that we must meet again soon. We set the time for an afternoon later in the week, when she would come to tea to see our new lodgings and tell me all about the accommodations in the new dormitory.

At that point, I should have guessed the anticipation I felt for the meeting would only lead to disappointment. It seemed everything I did those days ended in failure and frustration.

The first thing that happened that afternoon was that my brother appeared unexpectedly, with Teddy Hanover in tow. I was outraged. My mother and I had shopped for cold meats, bread and a lemon cake in the expectation that we three women would be alone. I had mentioned Clara's visit to Alden but he was never at home at that hour of the day. Contrary to all expectations he walked in, jauntily leading his companion.

My mother welcomed them and quickly directed Alden to move chairs from the dining area into our tiny parlor. It gave me some relief to see that Mr. Hanover had at least left behind his huge top hat but he wore an alarming suit in a loud plaid wool of greens and yellows. It appeared a little too small for his frame and his bony wrists shot out at the cuffs. He had a shaggy mop of dirty hair with large sideburns and settled himself into the most comfortable chair in the room, looking around with a big grin.

"So, these are your new digs. Alden told me they were topping. It must be great for you being so close to the Midway and the university, too," he told me with an obvious confidence that I would take his remarks as a compliment. "Aldy says it's a real bargain to boot, didn't you, Aldy? The landlord got stuck when some foreign exhibitor packed up early like, is that it?"

I endeavored to hide my surprise that he would make such a tactless remark about something so personal as our finances but I caught my brother's eye and glared at him.

"That's right," Alden agreed, shrugging his shoulders at me in a sign of nonchalance. "It was a great bargain. My sister has started classes again at the university and staying with us she can save on board as well." He made a face at me behind his friend's back. He knew I must object to discussion of such matters with a relative stranger. He was purposely trying to provoke me but my mother began to pour the tea and attempted to smooth the waters.

"We are happy to be able to spend more time with Emily. Alden and I missed her dreadfully last year. Being together again as a family this summer has been very comforting. Please help yourself to some cake, Mr. Hanover. Miss Clara Shea, a friend of my daughter's, will be joining us any minute now but we will not stand on ceremony to wait for her, as she is a very dear friend and will not mind."

Suddenly I could see that Teddy Hanover became aware that his manners were in doubt. My mother had served him first and that seemed to embarrass him.

"I thank you very much, Mrs. Cabot. When Alden told me to come along to tea I thought he was joking. I told him you'd not be wanting us horning in on your party but he insisted."

"That's right. I did insist and we're hungry." My brother took a slice of cake for himself and attacked it with all the greediness of a child. Poor Teddy Hanover still looked uncomfortable and it made me angry at Alden for putting the young man in such a position.

"Certainly, we are pleased that you could join us, Mr. Hanover," I told him, relenting on my own impulse to put him at ease. "My mother and I have tea most afternoons but it is unusual for Alden to join us. He seems to spend all of his time at the Midway these days. Though I'm sure I don't know what he's doing."

I was rewarded by a spark of gratitude in the young man's eyes and he accepted a piece of cake with a returning grin.

"My sister spends all her time pouring over old books," Alden jibed, pointing to a stack on the table by the door. "She can't imagine that anyone else could be learning new things in any other way than by reading them off the printed page. I'll get it."

He sprang up to answer a knock on the door that no one else had even heard and, a moment later, there were voices in the hallway. Teddy looked down at his plate of food with an uncharacteristically modest gaze. So that was it. It wasn't hunger that drew the young men to our party, it was the prospect of seeing my beautiful friend. I raised an eyebrow at my mother but she seemed amused.

That my younger brother should take an interest in Clara seemed very unlikely to me. Clara was my age and Alden was several years younger. It has been my observation that men will feel obliged to demonstrate an active interest in a fine looking woman no matter how unlikely it may be that anything will come of it. I knew Clara was accustomed to receiving such admiration but I thought it typically exasperating of my brother to indulge it at that moment.

Clara entered, followed by Alden. She was looking lovely, her cheeks slightly reddened by the October breeze.

"Look what I found," Alden announced as if she were unexpected. I might have scolded him but I could see Clara enjoyed his teasing. We introduced Mr. Hanover, whose presence was truly a surprise to Clara, as I could see. She managed to hide it, ducking her head as she sat down and we got everyone settled with teacups and plates of food.

"You're both students, then, are you?" Teddy asked in an obvious effort at acceptable conversation. The men seemed to come to attention at Clara's entrance. They were much more willing to exert themselves to please now. "Studying for degrees and such, are you?"

Clara and I exchanged a glance but I quickly looked away, knowing that we might break into laughter if we held it and that it would embarrass poor Mr. Hanover.

"Actually, Miss Shea and I have both already received college degrees. We are currently engaged in graduate study." Teddy's look of incomprehension required a fuller description of the type of work we were engaged in and the Englishman was obviously amazed at the very idea of it.

"Do you mean to say, a beautiful lady like yourself, Miss Shea, spends time mixing up nasty chemical concoctions while you, Miss Cabot, count all the horrible crimes in the city? Whatever would you want to do that for?"

Alden nearly choked with laughter and he patted his friend on the back. "An excellent question, Teddy. It's what I ask my sister all the time and she has yet to come up with a rational answer."

"Just because you fritter away your days with no purpose whatsoever," I told him severely, "you can hardly expect the rest of the world to be so dilettante. There is important research going on at the university as you are very well aware, Alden. Don't be misleading Mr. Hanover. The type of thing that is done here can lead to practical advances in the long run, Mr. Hanover, I assure you."

"That is true," Clara agreed with me. "Some of the work in biology is especially promising. There is hope they may find the causes of diseases, for instance." Inevitably that reminded me of Dr. Chapman and I felt a wave of pity for him, as we sat drinking tea in this pleasant room, while he was in a prison somewhere in the dark city. I put down my plate and looked at Clara. From her expression I knew she was thinking of him as well.

"Is there any news of Dr. Chapman, Emily? He is a friend of ours, Mr. Hanover. He has had the terrible misfortune to be charged with murder."

"Oh, aye. He's the chappie they took in for shooting that man Larrimer, isn't he?"

"We are most distressed by his troubles," my mother told him. "We owe Dr. Chapman a great deal since he treated my daughter when she was dangerously ill."

"Aye, Alden told me about that. It sounds an awful close call. But you think he didn't do it, this Dr. Chapman, is that it? I heard he was in love with the man's wife or some such. Perhaps this Larrimer attacked him if he was jealous, then?" He sounded like he was trying to be helpful.

"Well, hardly," Alden injected as he reached for another slice of cake. "Larrimer was shot in the back. But we don't think the doctor did it all the same, do we?"

"Certainly not," I snapped.

"I heard they never found the gun, anyhow," Teddy volunteered.

"Unfortunately they charged him with the crime despite the fact that they found no gun," I said. Then, looking at Clara, I continued, "Apparently they will hold off on the trial until after the Fair ends. The university has hired a lawyer and everyone who knows the doctor has volunteered to testify on his behalf. He is greatly valued here and no one can believe he could have done this dreadful thing. But there is a great fear that the city officials are prejudiced against him and they will seek to end the matter with a quick conviction. It is fearful to think they could very well condemn him with so little real evidence."

" 'Tis seen as a crime of passion," Teddy explained, as if he had knowledge in these matters. "That's always the simplest explanation of all. They have evidence he was in love with the wife, I hear. He was even engaged to her at one time, wasn't he?"

"But that was years ago," I protested, then realized how inappropriate it sounded that I should know so much of his personal affairs. "Even her father said as much to Alden and me. There is some suspicion there was something else going on. You yourself warned Alden to stay away from the Midway that night, Mr. Hanover, didn't you?"

Teddy swallowed a large gulp of tea and returned the china cup to its saucer with a great deal of care. "Well, yes, but that was nothing after all."

"You made it sound like more than nothing at the time," Alden pointed out.

"Oh, well, I was just trying to scare you. It was just a bunch of toughs like we're always getting down there."

As long as we were on the topic, it seemed to me I should learn as much as I could from the wily barker. "It has been suggested that Mr. Larrimer might have threatened to expose a gambling den that the police suspected was located somewhere on the Midway and that the operator might have shot him to keep him quiet," I said.

"Well, now, I'd find that hard to believe, Miss Cabot. Not that there isn't a game of chance or two going on and not that there aren't folks trying to make money off them and trying to keep it secret from the police and all, but they wouldn't go shooting Larrimer. Why should they?"

Alden was unnaturally silent through all of this but he raised no objection to my attempts to interrogate his friend. It suddenly occurred to me that his motive for bringing Teddy to tea had been that he wanted him probed, but did not particularly want to do it himself. I brushed aside the thought and continued.

"Not even to avoid exposure?"

"But why would he expose them? From what I heard his own father-in-law was into some of those games."

"But that might be a reason, might it not? Especially if he were pressed to pay Dr. Ramsey's debts."

Teddy frowned. "There now, he paid up on them though."

"To Mr. Marco?"

"That's right."

"Are you quite sure he really did pay? If he refused and threatened to expose the gambling instead, what might happen?"

"Oh, well, if that's what you want to know, I can tell you he paid up all right. Marco showed me the bills. But if you want to know what was bothering Mr. Larrimer, you might want to talk to your friend, Fitz. They were tight, Fitz and him. Fitz had him under his wing so to speak. It was Fitz as brought him down to the Midway, him and Dr. Ramsey, and Fitz as introduced them around. Now you're very friendly with that gentleman from the city, Miss Cabot. He has a great admiration for you, I'd say. If you've got questions about Mr. Larrimer, he's the man to ask."

I felt myself flush at this interpretation. Mr. Fitzgibbons indeed. Clara suppressed a smile at the idea that Mr. Fitzgibbons admired me. And I could see that Alden was terribly amused by the thought.

"You are wrong, Mr. Hanover. Mr. Fitzgibbons is a very recent acquaintance. It was in an effort to help Dr. Chapman that

I consulted him and it was his suggestion that we go to see Mr. Marco to attempt to find out what was going on the night Mr. Larrimer was killed."

Alden smiled, enjoying my discomfort at his friend's outrageous assumption of intimacy between myself and Mr. Fitzgibbons. But Teddy was regarding me quite seriously, his mouth slightly open, as he concentrated on understanding what I was saying.

"You mean to say," he asked with a frown, "you dragged old Fitz down to put old Marco on the spot like, because you wanted to help this Dr. Chapman?" He shook his head and continued without waiting for a reply. "That Fitz, he's a powerful fellow, you know. He's got a lot of power in the city—a lot of connections. Sounds like your friend the doctor is not near so well connected. He may not have shot the man, but it sounds like he's for it anyways, Miss Cabot. Better give him up, you had. It's a sorry business once you're in the hands of the police." He spoke as if from personal experience. "You'll do better with Fitz, you know. He told Alden here how much he admired you, didn't he?"

My brother nodded. "Said she was a great dancer, 'light as a mist on a summer's day' was how he put it."

I glared at Alden. "You misunderstand, Mr. Hanover. Dr. Chapman is a dear friend who is in trouble. We will do anything in our power to assist him. We would not abandon him just when he is most in need of his friends."

I thought poor Teddy looked stunned at this rebuke, but my mother and Clara agreed and even my brother concurred.

"But Teddy is right, too," Alden insisted. "If you want to help Dr. Chapman, you should go to Fitz. He has influence with the city. Oh, don't be a prig, Emily. He likes you. You want to help your friend, so use that."

"Detective Whitbread is assisting with the investigation," I replied. I did not mention the detective's troubles with Fitz and the city but I explained how he had been sent to investigate the possibility of a lynching that Mr. Larrimer might have been involved in some years previously. Teddy listened with rapt attention.

"You mean you think Larrimer got a mob together and took the man from jail and hung him?" The idea of lynch law was new to him. I told him that was what was being investigated. "Wicked," he said. "A wicked deed. That Larrimer was a bad one, then. If he would do a thing like that there's no telling who might have it in for him. Maybe that will help your friend, Dr. Chapman."

"But time is running out, Emily," my brother told me. "If Whitbread doesn't find anything in time, Chapman will go to trial and be railroaded. You still should go and see Fitzgibbons. He might be able to do something."

He shook his head then clapped Teddy on the back. "We had better be on our way. I promised Marco I'd get you back in plenty of time for the night crowds. Come on. We've intruded on my sister's party long enough. She'll throw us out if we don't behave ourselves." He turned to Clara. "But the Fair will be over soon, Miss Shea. You must come and ride the Ferris Wheel one more time before they take it apart and cart it away."

Clara smiled. "That will be a sad day, Mr. Cabot. But I must attend to my studies now. There is not much time for amusements once classes have started."

"Well, you must let me know if you change your mind." He stood up and Teddy joined him. Stepping towards Clara, Alden boldly extended his hand. She took it with a smile.

"Thank you, ladies," Teddy told us with a big bow. "Wonderful cake."

"Now that you have found us, Mr. Hanover, you must come to see us again," my mother told him.

"Yes," I said. "Don't rely on Alden. When you feel the need for a lovely tea, just remind him and come along." I said it mainly to annoy my brother but Teddy Hanover replied with unexpected grace.

"Why, thank you, Miss Cabot. I've enjoyed myself very much, I can tell you. At home, you know, university people like you would never sit down to tea with the likes of me."

He bowed again and was gone.

My mother, knowing my motives only too well, raised an eyebrow in my direction as she followed to let them out. I sighed. Soon she returned and stood in the doorway.

"Miss Shea, I have been having a wonderful correspondence with your grandmother. Since you all left we have exchanged several letters. She is a very accomplished woman."

"She was very pleased to make your acquaintance, too, Mrs. Cabot. She mentioned it several times on the journey home."

"Now, if you will excuse me for a few minutes, I know you both have much to catch up on and I will just prepare another pot of tea."

Taking up the china pot, she headed to the kitchen and Clara moved to a chair by my side.

"Emily, I have had a most distressing letter from my mother." She fumbled in her bag and brought out a folded paper. "I would not have you take offense. Detective Whitbread's investigations have stirred up a hornet's nest." She hesitated then extended her hand with the letter. I took it from her.

"It's best if you read it yourself, so you may see what I mean."

It was a heavy paper written over with a delicate script in purple ink. I found the sentiments it contained less than delicate, however.

Daughter Clara,

It is with anger in my heart that I take up my pen to tell you in no uncertain terms that you must return home immediately. I will not consent to allow a daughter of mine to remain in a place where her associations can bring nothing but disgrace to herself, her family and all her friends.

We have had a letter from Dr. Ramsey protesting the actions of a detective from Chicago who has appeared in Sherville and proceeds to incite trouble and bring great grief to our already stricken friends there. He informs us that the man has been sent by a group of insolent, scheming Negroes, and your friend Miss Cabot, to spread vicious lies concerning Marguerite Larrimer and even her poor dead husband who can no longer defend himself. That you should be in any way associated with persons of such low breeding and vile intent brings disgrace to us all. As your mother I demand that you immediately return to your home where you may hope to live up to a heritage of civility unknown in your current location. At least here there is some remnant of civilized life which may resist the onslaught of brutality that festers in places such as the city you now inhabit. I will not allow a daughter of mine to become polluted by such society.

It pains me to be forced to write of such matters and it goes against my very nature and upbringing to have to mention them. Your friends, it seems, have discovered a dark secret and seek to drag it into public view to the disgrace of a woman already greatly wronged and her husband dead at the murdering hands of a man whom they would have released on the basis of these lies.

It is not insignificant that the vicious assault Marguerite Larrimer suffered has been termed the 'usual crime.' You know very well that ever since the North released the slaves to a condition of idleness with no control—subject to no authority—that there has been an epidemic of such insults against Southern women. And you know very well it is not in the nature of any gentleman to allow such a grievous insult to go unanswered. That a man should have defended his wife's honor, only to be condemned for it after he can no longer defend himself, is too great an injury to be sustained. As your mother I forbid you to associate with people who would consent to such an insult.

I have no doubt that there are those who remain in Sherville who will deal with the offenses of this insolent intruder from the North who dares to attempt to defame the dead. But I know that, at the place where you are now, any lie or deceit that maligns the South will be believed. We, who preserve the remnants of that good and civil society that once existed, can only protest by refusing to associate with such scum. So I would have you break off your associations with your sanctimonious Northern friends and return to your home immediately. I will brook no argument on this and demand your obedience.

Your mother,

Julia Devereaux Shea

I flushed at the picture of myself as I appeared to Clara's mother. Clara reached across and squeezed my arm.

"You must forgive me for making you read that, but I think you should know what reaction may be provoked by digging up the past. You see that it is perceived as a great wrong done to Marguerite Larrimer if you attempt to uncover the story of her disgrace. People take offense that anyone should feel so little pity for a woman who has already suffered and must now bear her husband's death. To make public the fact that she was defiled is to wrong her in their eyes. Furthermore, there seems some threat to Detective Whitbread if he pursues his investigation. Feeling runs very deep against it."

"But, Clara, what about Dr. Chapman? Would you have him convicted of a crime he did not commit? The intention is not to malign Mrs. Larrimer or to cause her any pain. The intention is only to find the truth."

"Sometimes the truth can be very ugly, Emily. And it may not help the doctor at all. There is no reason to believe whatever happened is in any way connected to Mr. Larrimer's death. How could it be?"

"But someone connected to the man who was lynched was seen by Mr. Larrimer. It is that person we seek. Whoever it was may have a motive for revenge stronger than any perceived motive of Dr. Chapman. Do you not see that?"

Clara sighed. "It seems unlikely. It is not usual for there to be any revenge in such cases, at least I have never heard of it. The man is condemned by all for such savage behavior. Even the Negroes find your friend Miss Wells too strident in her protests against such actions."

"But they must be afraid of reprisals. How could they not be when such things are allowed to happen? My father was a judge, Clara. He taught me to respect the workings of the law. There must be provision for fair trial or there can be no justice. Society cannot allow private revenge. Law must prevail or we will all be reduced to savagery."

"But the law does not always result in justice, Emily. Is it just that a woman already wronged should be disgraced in public? Now, you are afraid that a court of law will unjustly convict Dr. Chapman. In the case of Mr. Larrimer, he may have believed a court of law would have released the Negro who attacked his wife. I do not want to defend the action, only to explain it. And to drag out poor Marguerite's disgrace into public view, either then or now, is seen as another wrong against her. I do not think even a Northern jury would have sympathy for a man who would subject a woman to such public disgrace to save his own neck. Think of it. You may be doing the doctor great harm by pursuing this. Do you really think he would wish it?"

I could not answer this, for I knew in my heart he would not have this line of inquiry pursued.

"And there is another thing, Emily. You say the truth must be found. But what if it is not to your liking? As much as you and I have enjoyed the company of Dr. Chapman and found him a good and upright man, we know so little about him. Even good men may be the victims of their passions. He did love Marguerite once. Passion and jealousy can be overwhelming emotions in men, Emily. And even if we had known the doctor to be a gentle soul for more years than we have, how could we say with certainty that passion might not erupt in him and result in violence? It seems to me there was a strong feeling between him and Marguerite Larrimer. We cannot know the depths of it or what he may have been capable of under its influence."

There came unbidden to my mind the picture of Dr. Chapman on the portico of the Music Hall and I heard him once again condemn Mr. Larrimer. "No. I do not believe it. He disliked, maybe even hated Larrimer. But I do not believe he would shoot the man in the back and then conceal the act."

"But, perhaps admitting it would only bring more disgrace on Marguerite and he holds his tongue to spare her. Have you considered that?"

"Oh, Clara, how can you think that?"

My mother entered then carrying a full teapot but Clara stood up. She looked a little pale.

"Mrs. Cabot, I thank you very much but you must excuse me now, as I must be going."

"I'm sorry you cannot stay longer, Clara, but I hope you will return to see us soon."

"I believe my studies will demand my attention for some time before I will be able to visit here again," she said stiffly, and I saw she had her own battle before her. I longed to assure her of my help but held my tongue. After all, it was association with me to which her mother objected so strongly and we were far from agreement on the rightness of my actions, now or in the future. So, I let her go with only a stiff goodbye.

My mother gave me a worried look and showed Clara to the door. When she returned I fell to weeping and confessed the contents of the letter. I was sure it would be some time, if ever, before we would see Clara Shea again.

SIXTEEN

*T*he end of the week was dismal and rainy. The force of the downpour brought down the last remaining leaves from the trees and they lay in soggy masses between pools of mud around the half-completed buildings of the campus. Even the White City lost its festive air when seen through a curtain of rain as I slogged my way to the Haitian pavilion, only to be disappointed in the lack of news from Detective Whitbread.

As a diversion I impulsively decided to attempt a visit to Mr. Fitzgibbons. I had no confidence in my brother's belief that, owing to his position in the city, Mr. Fitzgibbons could have some influence on Dr. Chapman's trial. But I was desperate to try any avenue since we seemed to be mired down, while time marched on inevitably to that much feared day when the trial would begin.

Telling no one of my plan, I took a train downtown and found my way to City Hall where many inquiries eventually led me to an office down a dingy hallway in the corner of the ground floor. There I found a weedy looking young man at the desk who said he was Mr. Fitzgibbons's secretary. He regarded me with ill-disguised speculation when I requested an interview and begged me to take a seat on the hard bench along the wall. Mr. Fitzgibbons was in a conference and would have to be consulted after its conclusion to ascertain whether or not he was available. He intended to impress me with his boss's importance and heavy load of duties. I confess it did make me doubt the value of my errand but having come thus far I decided to wait on chance.

I sat long enough to become uncomfortable on the hard wood when the wide door to the inner office opened and Mr. Fitzgibbons stood with his back to me, ushering out his visitor, who I saw was Mr. Prendergast. Fitzgibbons was speaking and, by his tone, I judged him to be displeased with the man. Fitz held some postcards in his hand, which he waved in the air as he motioned the man to leave. "We'll have no more of this then, is that clear? No more of this nonsense about the corporation counsel. You're not fit for it, man, and that's the end of it."

"It was promised me." Mr. Prendergast had a squeaky voice and a frown upon his face.

"Are you daft, man? I said a place will be found for you and it will. But you must stop pestering the mayor and those around him." He flapped the postcards in the other man's face. "No more of these, do you hear me? If you have something to say you will come to me, man to man, and say it."

"I have done great deeds for the machine. I will have my due."

"What, would you threaten us then? We'll have no more talk of your deeds. You do what you're told and you'll be taken care of. You know that's how it works, man."

"I was promised."

"Will you go on, then?" Fitz sounded exasperated. "Just get it into your thick skull that you will have your place. But stay out of the counsel's office, now."

"They made a joke of it. They ridiculed me. I won't be made ridiculous."

"Then don't be making a fool of yourself, for God's sake. You've no law degree, and no education to speak of. We've already been over this. You go now and do as you're bid or you won't have any place here and I'll see to it you're blackballed from getting a place anywhere in this city. No more of this now. Go."

They glared at each other but Prendergast let his eyes fall first. I was surprised by the look of hatred in them for the brief moment I witnessed. He slouched out however, and Fitz turned to his secretary.

"God preserve us from fools."

The secretary had nodded in my direction to warn him of my presence and he became suddenly aware of me. The slightest look of confusion crossed his face but he greeted me warmly.

"Miss Cabot, what brings you here on such a gloomy, dreary day?"

I was aware of him looking me up and down and I knew the bits of mud caked on my hem and boots did me no credit.

"I'm sorry to disturb you, Mr. Fitzgibbons, but I hoped to discuss a matter with you. I was not sure of where to write, so I came myself. If the time is not convenient, I thought I might arrange an appointment at a more suitable hour."

Faced with the man in the flesh, I felt my spirit quailing and cursed myself for stumbling over such a long speech. He gave me a searching look as if to delve into my motives but I think he was unsuccessful.

"Well now, since you've come such a long way we don't want to send you back empty handed." He turned to the secretary, "John, would you just trot over to Barney Henson and tell him I'll be a few minutes late, then." He gestured to the door, "Come in, Miss Cabot. Sorry to keep you waiting like that."

It was a big square room with high molded ceilings and large windows looking down on a busy street, as if he might never be too far removed from the people passing back and forth across the city. One side was taken up by a large fireplace and a group of chairs and couches. I had the impression it must be the site of many a meeting. He led me to the other side, where a large desk sat facing the windows, with two padded leather chairs opposite him for visitors. He helped me to one of the chairs and took the armchair behind the desk, which was piled high with paper forms and newspapers. On the wall above hung a large portrait of Mayor Carter Harrison and flag stands stood on either side. One held the Stars and Stripes, while the other held the flag of the city of Chicago.

On a sideboard against the wall a number of photographs in frames were displayed. There was one of what must have been a St. Patrick's Day celebration with Fitz and Mayor Harrison raising beer mugs in salute to a surrounding crowd of people. Another was of the White City of the Exposition and the final one was a group picture of a dozen or so people of a span of ages. Fitz stood beside a gray haired woman and on the other side stood a woman in a wedding dress with other men and women and children all gathered around. It was a family portrait. He noticed my glance had stopped at it and reached over and took it up in his hand.

"My family. It's a large lot." He turned it towards me. "That's me mother—our father died a long time ago and she's had the raising of all nine of us. This was at my brother James's wedding. That's Mary Elizabeth Corcoran that was, a fine girl. They have a baby daughter now and another on the way." He shook his head. "It's a fine thing seeing as she was my girl first. But I was too busy campaigning and James won her away from me. More's the pity. But it's all in the family and I'm the one got him the job as a fireman." He turned away to set the photograph carefully back in its place.

"I'm sorry you had to overhear that little fracas with Prendergast, Miss Cabot. Those that work in the political campaign of the mayor get a lot of notions about what's owed them. And many have skills we can draw on and put them in the best position as is good for both them and the city. And there's others who have more dreams and schemes than skills and it's harder to place them. Now Mr. Prendergast is one that has lots of ideas but most of them aren't practical a bit. He can't seem to get it into his head that he cannot be legal counsel if he's never even read the law." He shook his head again. "But, there, we'll find the right spot for him in the end."

"Mr. Lowry at the university says it is one of the evils of the political patronage system that those who are most competent for jobs may be passed over in favor of those with political connections while others, like Mr. Prendergast, are led to aspire to positions for which they are unsuited and may become resentful when given a lesser place."

His attitude towards me shifted slightly then and I realized too late that he perceived this statement as a criticism. I could just picture my brother Alden shaking his head at my lack of tact. But it was Alden who encouraged me to come to Fitz in the first place and I had a sinking feeling now that it was a great mistake. Fitz sat back in his chair and considered me with a blank expression on his face. I felt I did not recognize him at all.

"Luckily enough, Miss Cabot, Mayor Harrison attracts to him many supporters who are very competent to handle the job of running a great city. The success of the Fair is only one example. Now it may be that your professors at the university think they could do a better job but they will never be in a position to prove it. And I'll tell you why." He leaned forward. "They would never be elected by the people. They've a great knowledge of the learning in books but they've no knowledge at all of the trials and tribulations of the people. It's getting jobs for the great mass of people that is the goal of the politician. It's not the swells on Prairie Avenue or the scholars at the university who need looking after by the state, you see. It's all them people struggling to exist out there."

He pointed to the street crowds below the window. "They're the people who need a mayor who will find more jobs and help them in their struggle and they're the people who elected him. So, who should be surprised if, after giving him their vote, they think they can come to him and bring their troubles and ask him to help them? And that's the kind of mayor he is. His door is always open and there are always those in search of help who come knocking and he's always there to listen and do something if he can."

He was looking hard at me to see if I understood. I almost expected him to tell me to get that through my thick head, but he sat back again and smiled. "And the same is true of his administration, so what can I do for you, Miss Cabot? It seems to me you must have some suit to have come all the way down here from the university to find me out."

I was embarrassed. Of course, I had come to him looking for assistance and it made me in some way as much a supplicant as Mr. Prendergast. I wished I had never taken Alden's advice in this.

"As you know, we ... Mr. Reed, my professor, and I ... have been compiling a study of crime in the city. Detective Whitbread was assisting us." I glanced at him, remembering our last meeting and how he had been the one to tell the detective of his forced transfer. He returned my gaze steadily. "Since he has been transferred, we have had difficulty getting cooperation. We've written to the commission but received no response. There are other files we wish to consult but we are unable to find anyone who can help us. Is there anything you could do to assist us? Might we not again work with Detective Whitbread, who was so sympathetic to our approach?"

He leaned forward and made a note on a pad of paper. "We would certainly want to assist you in your study," he said. "I believe it would be possible for someone to be assigned to look out the records you are seeking and allow you access to them. I will speak to Al Corbett, who is assistant to the commissioner. No doubt the press of day-to-day business in dealing with crime has kept them from responding. I'm sure they will be amenable to your study." He dropped the pencil. "As for Henry Whitbread, I'm afraid that is another matter. It seems he lodged a formal protest against the transfer and then left town." He looked directly at me. "I received a complaint from Dr. Ramsey. Apparently Whitbread has shown up in Sherville and claims to be investigating an incident of some years past. I assured Dr. Ramsey that he is not pursuing any legitimate police investigation."

"He is on leave," I blurted out, and saw a look of calculation cross his face as the statement confirmed his suspicion that I knew of the detective's errand. "He was asked to investigate a lynching that took place in Sherville five years ago. Mr. Larrimer was involved. It is possible that incident might provide the true motive for Mr. Larrimer's murder."

"He's working for Chapman's attorney?"

"No." I was suddenly conscious of my foolishness. I had no idea whether I should be telling Fitzgibbons about these matters but I had begun and must continue. "He was hired by a committee of the local Negro community. They investigate and compile details of these incidents of lynching."

"It's Barnett, then."

I was surprised by his knowledge but I should not have been. He must always be aware of whatever went on in the city. "And Miss Ida B. Wells. She arranged for the publication and distribution of a pamphlet describing the problem."

"I am aware of the pamphlet. It is unfortunate for Whitbread that he has taken on this task. I understand a hearing on his complaint has been scheduled. If he does not appear, it will be dismissed and the fact that he would bring such a complaint will be held against him, I'm afraid. I will not be able to ask for him to be assigned to help you, Miss Cabot. I am very much afraid that he and the department will part company altogether as a result of this latest action."

"But that is unfair. As I understand it, he had leave owed him. He is working on his own time."

"But he is seen as a representative of this city's police department and he is embarrassing that department. It will not end well, Miss Cabot."

"But he is only looking for the truth of the incident. It seems certain a man was taken out and hung illegally in Sherville."

"It is not Sherville, Kentucky that interests us, Miss Cabot. It is Chicago. Whitbread should be here in Chicago. There will be no lynchings in Chicago. But we must have our officers here to maintain the peace and order—not running off to other states to tell them what they are doing wrong. It is the people here," again he pointed out the window, "in this city, that Detective Whitbread should be protecting."

"But there is a very great danger that—here in this city—you may convict the wrong man for the murder of Mr. Larrimer. Dr. Chapman is unfairly accused. Someone shot Mr. Larrimer but it was not the doctor. How can you discover who really did it if you will not investigate others who might have had reason to hate him?"

He put a hand up and rubbed his forehead. "You are loyal to your friend, Miss Cabot. I admire that. And Larrimer was not a nice man. Believe me, I could see that. He saw that pamphlet of Miss Wells and he wanted us to suppress it, as if we should take sides with him against some of our own people. For Barnett and his people are their own force in Chicago, let me tell you. Larrimer was no better than the rich swells of this city who want us to step on the poor working man whenever he rises up." He made a face of disgust. "But they have to be humored, if only so far. And Larrimer treated his wife badly. Whatever may have happened to her in the past, he had no business insulting her by visiting prostitutes in the Levee. But men are like that, Miss Cabot, as you may not realize. And you may not understand that if a man like your friend Dr. Chapman saw the way Larrimer was treating a woman that he himself had been in love with, he might well take it upon himself to stop it. He was found standing over the dead man, the jealous lover over the unworthy husband. I am sorry, Miss Cabot. He did it and he will have to pay for it. We may all sympathize with him, and not regret the deed perhaps, but for the sake of peace in the community it cannot go unpunished."

I felt a lump in my throat. This was what they all believed and he made the result sound so final and inevitable. I had no heart to argue the lack of the gun, or the motives of others. Who would listen to me? It was so appalling to hear him say it all so bluntly and he was so adamant in his conviction. I gathered my skirts and stood to leave. Coming at all had been a mistake. He stood up, also.

"You are wrong, Mr. Fitzgibbons. If Dr. Chapman had done what you believe, he would have admitted it. I thank you for your time."

"I am very sorry, Miss Cabot."

I did not respond but continued quickly out the door and through the sprawling corridors peopled all with men, talking in earnest conversation or lounging against posts, waiting to make their suits. I didn't stop until I reached the outside where throngs of people hurried along. The rain was coming down heavily now and they were bent over beneath umbrellas, or hunched with coats pulled up to their ears.

It had been a mistake to come to Fitzgibbons. Alden and Teddy had been wrong. I had no influence with that gentleman. His care was only for the machinations of city politics which, he believed, kept this swarm of humanity alive and mobile. To him, Dr. Chapman was an obstacle to be removed in the interest of the greater aims of the city administration. It must not be said that the Southern visitor could be murdered in this city without retribution and it seemed that Dr. Chapman's life was required to settle that debt. And now Detective Whitbread was in danger of losing his job for daring to go against the plans of City Hall. What had I done? Once again in my naiveté I had been the cause of great damage. I determined I must go to Miss Wells and ask her to recall Whitbread so he might tend to his own affairs before his life was ruined as well. But I stood for a moment. I had dressed in my best summer suit with my finest hat, all of which was about to be ruined by a plunge into the pouring rain. Nothing more than I deserved for such foolishness, I told myself.

"Miss Cabot."

I jumped. I was at the front of the building before the tall doors. I had stopped at the top of the marble stairs but I was so engrossed by my thoughts and self-recriminations I was oblivious to the figure who had come up quite close behind me.

"Mr. Prendergast, I did not see you." I would have moved away from him but he was so close I could only step forward, which would put me in the rain. "Excuse me." I slid sideways and turned to face him.

At such close quarters, I could see he was a tall thin young man only a few years older than me. He had dark hair cut quite short and gray eyes that seemed to remain open without blinking. Above a long thin neck with a prominent Adam's apple he was clean-shaven except for a small dark moustache that somehow looked false. He was very gawky with jerky movements that reminded me of a marionette and his tendency to creep close to you and peer at you intensely was disconcerting. I remembered the look of hatred he had aimed at Fitz and I was wary.

"Miss Cabot. Seen Fitzgibbons, haven't you?" Again he took a step closer to me and I instinctively stepped back to put some distance between us. I felt distressed by the rudeness of this but I could not help it and he seemed not to notice.

"Yes."

"He wouldn't help, would he?" He was nodding his head without waiting for me to reply. "You wrote letters for Whitbread. He doesn't like it. They can't be completely ignored though. There are others who are impressed." He chuckled. "Fitz can't stand it but there's nothing he can do. He wouldn't help you, though, would he? You want to help the doctor who's been arrested, don't you? That's why you came. Right?"

"I . . . yes . . . I do want to help Dr. Chapman. I am very much afraid he will be condemned for something he didn't do."

He looked over his shoulder and back. "Maybe I can help you. Yes, I can help you. But not here." He took my elbow and pushing his umbrella open with the other hand he urged me down the steps, glancing right and left as if to make sure we wouldn't be seen. This time I did not pull away. Something about this very intense young man made me uncomfortable but he had been there the night of Larrimer's death soon after the man was found and it seemed possible that he had seen something. He quickly led me around a corner and into a dingy teashop where it appeared that he was known.

As he hurried me to a corner table he flapped his long arms in large gestures to convey orders to a man in a white apron who responded with a raised eyebrow, but nodded at a waitress to follow us. Prendergast busied himself with pulling out a chair for me and sweeping out another for himself. It was all very awkward and embarrassing. It occurred to me that this gawky young man was not in the habit of coming in with a young woman on his arm. When I noticed how he was preening himself as he sat opposite me, I thought of how Clara would use the knowledge to her advantage to get the young man's help but it only made me impatient to get to the issue.

"Mr. Prendergast, if you know something that could help to clear Dr. Chapman you must come forward and tell the authorities."

He looked away from me, his eyes darting around the room. We were interrupted by the waitress delivering a tray of cups and saucers and pouring a pot of tea. It was only when we were alone again that he leaned uncomfortably close and answered, "Maybe. It may be I know something . . . saw something." He sat back, glancing around again as if afraid we would be overheard.

"What is it, Mr. Prendergast? What do you know? Did you see something that night? Or somebody? You must say if you did."

"I might . . . might not. I am to take over as corporation counsel, did you know? But there's a hold up. But if you were to get university people to write letters for me, like for Whitbread, see . . . they'd have to take notice of those. They couldn't ignore those, you'll see."

"Mr. Prendergast, I don't know what you are talking about."

Now he was looking only at me with that unblinking stare as if he were trying to mesmerize me. "Letters. Letters like you wrote for Whitbread."

"But that was because we knew Detective Whitbread. We have been working with him for most of the year. I am sorry, Mr. Prendergast, but neither I nor anyone else at the university has any such knowledge of you or your qualifications for the job you seek. Really, I believe Mr. Fitzgibbons stated a degree in law is required and that you have nothing of the sort to offer."

"That's a ruse. It's all a trick. They have to say that because of him—Trask, the incumbent. He doesn't want to give it up and they haven't broken it to him. But it's all right. You'll see. Next week, Wednesday at the latest. The whole office will be mine. Most of the clerks can stay but there are a few who will have to go. You'll see."

By his fixed stare and earnest tone I could tell he was perfectly convinced of the truth of what he said. "But Mr. Prendergast, if that is the case you can hardly be in need of letters of recommendation. Please, won't you tell me what it is you know that would help Dr. Chapman?"

My plea only appeared to make him angry. "Tit for tat. Tit for tat, Miss Cabot. I help you if you help me. That's how it works. You know that. Everybody knows that."

"I know nothing of the sort. I cannot provide you with letters of recommendation for a job I know nothing about, Mr. Prendergast. If you know anything about the death of Mr. Larrimer you must tell the authorities."

He frowned at me. "That's not how it works. You don't know how it works."

I should have told him I would help him. His whole effort was so much an exercise in make-believe, I should have added make-believe letters for his make-believe job. But I couldn't do that. No doubt that was how the whole thing worked. Politicians, like Fitz, said yes to people like Prendergast or Larrimer or anyone from whom they needed something. They said yes to the job, yes to the contract, yes to the demand, then they never delivered. It was the way of it and Alden would say I was naïve to try to circumvent it with the truth. But I couldn't do it. Not even to this obviously deluded young man. Exasperated, I pulled some coins from my bag and dropped them on the table. It seemed to me this very unrealistic man probably would have some difficulty paying the bill. I slid from the seat. "I cannot help you, Mr. Prendergast, and you refuse to help me. Further discussion is useless. If you change your mind and want to tell me about what happened, you know where to find me."

With that I quickly strode from the room, pulling on my gloves as I went. There was something about the unwavering stare of the young man that made me uncomfortable and I was anxious to get away from him. Even my exit into the pouring rain, and the final destruction of my outfit, was preferable to continuing the useless argument. I had no doubt Prendergast had seen something that night, if only Marguerite Larrimer. I also had no doubt that, whatever it was, Fitz must know about it but neither one of them was likely to give up his secrets to me. We sorely needed Detective Whitbread to return before his own career was ruined. And I sorely needed his help in dealing with these men. I had made a mess of it. Both of them knew something but neither would cooperate. I realized how very, very foolish it had been to come. I needed Detective Whitbread—only he would be unable to extract the truth from these men.

SEVENTEEN

I hurried back to the fairgrounds and found Ida before she left for the day. When I explained the need to recall Detective Whitbread, she gave me a letter she had just received.

Dear Miss Wells,

As mentioned in my last report, it was necessary to await the close of Sunday services before I could again attempt to interrogate Mrs. Olivia Nokes and Mr. Thomas Smith concerning the lynching incident of 1886. It was only with the wholehearted assistance of Reverend Parsons, who invited those witnesses to his parlor, and who overcame their reluctance by a mighty appeal to their consciences, that we are able to have their stories which, as you shall see, differ greatly from the official accounts.

Mrs. Nokes has been cook at the Larrimer estate for her entire adult life. She was born to the place before the war which emancipated the slaves. Mr. Smith served as manservant to the dead Mr. Larrimer and he, too, has called the place home since his youngest days which may explain why they continued in service there, even after this terrible incident. One can only conjecture that over the many years of their service there, this was not the only act of cruelty which they have witnessed. It would seem over time they have learned a hard lesson and it has been their policy and necessity to out wait the malefactors in such crimes. With the death of Mr. Larrimer, that policy has succeeded yet still it is only with the greatest hesitation that they will tell their tale.

According to Mrs. Nokes, the Larrimer marriage was not a happy one. Soon after she took her place as his wife, Mrs. Larrimer realized what a mistake it had been to marry him. Unused to the accepted habits of such a man who kept a mistress, and was both demanding and critical of all those he claimed to possess, the young bride was soon miserable. A miscarriage, followed by the verdict that Mrs. Larrimer would never bear children, only widened the gap between husband and wife and they became barely civil in their mutual behavior.

It would seem that Mrs. Larrimer took refuge in her love of music and took it upon herself to encourage the talent of some of the Negro children on the estate. Mrs. Nokes clucked her tongue in disapproval at the memory of how Mrs. Larrimer discovered the abilities of one of the house servants, a young man of sixteen named William Jones. Despite a sure knowledge of her husband's disapproval, Mrs. Larrimer encouraged the young man, secretly teaching him first on her own piano and later on a violin, which she gave him and he soon mastered. As the husband was frequently away from home the boy became proficient under her tutelage.

But Mrs. Nokes, and others, saw the danger and she warned Miss Bessie Jones, the older sister of William and Robert. The sister could not persuade her brother to relinquish his studies and they all looked on with dismay as Mrs. Larrimer encouraged William to hope to pursue his studies away from the estate.

Both witnesses described an occasion when Mrs. Larrimer arranged for a concert for the servants while her husband was away. At her insistence, they were gathered in the parlor to hear William on the violin, while Mrs. Larrimer accompanied him on piano. When Mr. Larrimer returned unexpectedly there was an unpleasant scene and he had William whipped for this impertinence, despite the pleadings of his wife.

After that, William was sent to the fields and Mrs. Larrimer was forbidden to continue to give lessons to any of the children. The woman was devastated as she realized she was powerless to protest her husband's dictates.

It was at this time that Dr. Chapman paid a visit to the town. According to witnesses, Mrs. Larrimer's attitude then changed. While she ceased to oppose her husband openly—indeed she suffered his attitude of displaying her as a possession to the visitor in silence—Mrs. Nokes is convinced she planned to finally leave the man. She secretly packed a bag, and waited for her husband to leave on business the morning of September 24th, 1886. Mrs. Nokes saw this and was sure the woman left the house to make final arrangements to depart in secret with Dr. Chapman. But when she returned in the afternoon she was distraught and she demanded they send for William Jones from the fields. They were very reluctant to do this, fearing her husband would return and take his anger out on the boy. But she told them tearfully that she would be leaving and she wanted only to give William the violin and some money as a parting gift. They had the boy sent for. But, before he arrived, Mr. Larrimer returned. He found the bag she had packed and accused her of planning to elope with Chapman. He ordered the servants from the room and they listened to her cries and weeping as her husband hit her and hurled insults at her. He had never behaved in such a manner to her before and there was nothing they could do. Mrs. Nokes believes it was his fear and horror at the thought that his wife would really ever leave him that drove him out of his mind that day. He was such a proud man, it was beyond his comprehension.

Suddenly there was a pause and they were told William had come from the fields. Horrified that he would walk in on the scene, Mrs. Nokes and her fellow servants rushed to the parlor. They were too late. Larrimer had the boy pinned to the wall by his neck. On the floor, Mrs. Larrimer lay, her dress torn. Larrimer shouted that William had attacked his wife and would pay for it. Of course, none of them believed it. While they could not protest, Mr. Smith is sure that their very presence, silent though it was, but filling the room, prevented Larrimer from taking a pistol and shooting the young man then and there. Instead he knocked out the hapless William and ordered the servants to lock him in the icehouse and tend to Mrs. Larrimer. Then he ran from the house calling for his horse.

He returned an hour later with the sheriff, who took poor William away. Larrimer refused to allow anyone to talk to his wife, locking her in her room. Emotion ran high among the Negro population as the story circulated. The next morning the white editor of the newspaper wrote an editorial demanding retribution. Tension was high all day but the white employers were careful to see that none of their Negro employees were allowed out after sunset. Mr. Larrimer locked his own servants into the basement when he left that night.

The following morning they learned that William had been taken from the jail and lynched. The Reverend Parsons retrieved the body for proper burial but, even before that, friends of Bessie Jones had convinced her to take the younger boy, Robert, and flee. They took up a collection and smuggled them out of town. It is not known exactly where they fled but Mr. Smith tells me Bessie had an uncle in Pennsylvania, near Philadelphia.

Mrs. Larrimer took to her bed for some months following the incident and when she finally arose it was observed that her spirit was broken. Mrs. Nokes believes that ever after she was afraid of her husband and that Mr. Larrimer was so ashamed of what he had done that he forbade anyone to ever mention the incident in the future. They never saw such an outbreak of violence from him again.

I know that you will agree that the next step must be to find Bessie Jones and the younger brother. With this intention I leave for Philadelphia today by way of Louisville. You may reach me at the Hotel Biltmore. I believe at the very least we must be able to prove Mr. Larrimer was a man who made many enemies. It may be that we will uncover some relation or friend of Jones who has taken revenge. Thus do our deeds reap their harvest. I will write again on arrival.

Yours truly,

Henry Whitbread

"This was written three days ago. Surely there will be another soon. But we must wire him to return or his own case will be defaulted," I told Ida.

She seemed distracted and unhappy. Finally, she agreed but she said we must tell him of the circumstances and leave the decision to him. She would not outright dismiss him, but she promised to write to him that evening. I was turning to leave, thinking she seemed unusually unresponsive, when she called me back.

"Miss Cabot, I must ask your advice. I have received this."

She handed me a card elegantly inscribed with black ink. It was an invitation to a luncheon at the Palmer House the following Friday. It was from Clara's grandmother, Mrs. Shea.

"I am unsure how to respond," she told me. "I am not acquainted with that lady."

I explained that I was, and told her the particulars. She looked bemused.

"But why would this Southern lady invite me? I have frequently received invitations from ladies who have heard of our campaign and wish to support us," she told me. "And we are always grateful for such support. But this has always come from Northern or British ladies. This is the first time I have been solicited by a lady from the South and, I confess, I fear some insult is intended. I am very much afraid to accept this invitation lest I be subjected to some disagreeable situation. I don't know what she intends by it."

I sensed the fear she spoke of and, remembering Clara's grandmother, I could not believe it was justified. "I do not know what is meant by it, Ida, but my mother is friendly with Mrs. Shea and has been corresponding with her. I feel certain if she is in town and has planned such a luncheon we will also be invited. If that is the case, I think you may safely go with us for we would not submit to any insult being offered to you. I have not been home yet, but let me make sure we are also of the party and I will come tomorrow and tell you. Then we may all accept."

She looked relieved. "I would not like to refuse such an invitation if it is kindly meant," she told me. "But past experience, and threats that I have received personally, make me afraid of such an encounter."

I patted her arm. "I do not believe Mrs. Shea intends any harm. We must hope she is a convert, or at least that she may respect the motives that drive your campaign."

When I returned home I found we had been invited just as I expected and my mother agreed with me that Ida Wells should fear no insult by attending. We resolved to visit the young woman the next day to encourage her to attend and to promise our support and protection.

EIGHTEEN

Miss Wells, I am so glad you could join us today." Clara's grandmother took Ida's hand and held it in both of her own. The younger woman looked slightly flustered and dropped a little curtsy. "I must tell you how much I admire your efforts to stop these dreadful lynchings, my dear."

I saw Clara's eyes grow wide at this statement but her grandmother ignored her and addressed us all.

"I hope you will forgive me for rushing you all right in to the table but the delicacies are hot and we do not want them to spoil. So if you will just remove your hats, we'll sit down with no delay."

We followed her instructions, handing our hats to her Negro maid who grinned at me as if a visitor like Miss Wells was not an everyday occurrence. We entered a long room with green velvet drapes on the tall windows and satin upholstered couches and chairs. In front of the window a round table had been laid with silver and crystal and a waiter in white gloves stood by a cart holding covered dishes. We arranged ourselves around the table and I noticed the red cover of Ida's pamphlet where it lay prominently displayed.

"I have been having a most pleasant correspondence with your mother, Miss Cabot. But she told me with some regret that she feared you and Clara had had a misunderstanding. I think that would be most unfortunate, considering the fine friendship that has grown up between you."

My mother looked down at her plate demurely, while Ida looked up and her dark eyes darted between Clara and myself. Meanwhile the waiter was placing the plates of delicacies and small pots of tea around the table.

"I certainly regret any misunderstanding," I said, looking at Clara, but she avoided my eyes, concentrating on her food.

"I understand my granddaughter became heated in her defense of the honor of one of our friends." Mrs. Shea nodded. She tapped the red pamphlet that sat on the table in front of her. "I fear there has been much wrong done in the name of the honor of Southern ladies. Wouldn't you agree, Miss Wells?"

Ida nodded. But Clara had found her voice.

"Gram, what are you suggesting? Do you say it is wrong to defend the honor of white women who are attacked in the most vicious manner? Surely you do not condone that."

I saw Ida frown. Her dark eyes darted from face to face around the table and I saw her jaw set. I thought Mr. Barnett would have recognized the signs of an imminent outburst but Clara's grandmother spoke up first.

"Certainly not. I condone no violence against innocent persons. But, as you are so fond of pointing out, my dear, we must take a scientific approach. Miss Wells here has done that in her pamphlet, which you have not deigned to read. So, I think we must consult Miss Wells concerning her investigations and ask what she has discovered. It is true, is it not, Miss Wells, that in the majority of cases where a man has been lynched, based on the accusation that he assaulted a white woman, you found these accusations to be false?"

Ida sat straight-backed and sturdy, her hands folded in her lap. "Yes, Mrs. Shea, that is correct. In many cases, the man who is killed was not even accused of such an assault, and where such an accusation has been made, in most cases we have found no evidence of guilt. In some cases, the man hung is not even the one accused. In others, the supposed victim of the crime denies it, or denies any violence was involved. It is the Southern men, who have done these lynchings, who claim all Negro men have a propensity to attack white women. It is a myth they spread to excuse their own unlawful actions and we have sought to show that it is a myth wholly without foundation." Ida seemed unusually wary of the company. Her eyes narrowed. I had never seen her so little forthcoming before and I remembered her suspicions that the invitation held a threat of insult. She had come prepared to do battle. I thought she must have suffered insults in the past from women like Clara and her grandmother to be so tense and suspicious. I hoped my mother and I had not made a terrible mistake in encouraging her to come.

Mrs. Shea reached over and patted Ida's clasped hands. "This is true, Clara," she turned to her granddaughter, who had stopped eating. We all had. "I don't know where all this fear of the Negro has come from. Certainly it was not in evidence during the war when so many of us women were left behind with only our Negro menservants to protect us. Where was this great fear that we would be assaulted then?" She raised her eyebrows in emphasis. "You do remember Henry, Clara. Don't you?"

"Of course," Clara responded. She looked flustered.

"Of course." Mrs. Shea turned to the rest of us. "Henry was our butler and for two years during the war, while my husband and sons were away fighting, Henry and the other Negro servants were our only defense against the world. Far from being afraid of Henry and the others, we regarded them as our defenders. I must say, I miss Henry. We had many a talk in those days. I don't know what I would have done without him. After the war, he took his family to Oklahoma and settled there. I can't say that I blame him. We correspond, you know. Of course, Henry was never taught to read and write but his granddaughter writes for him. He says he is taking my advice and seeing to it that she will be educated."

Clara looked down at her plate.

"As for Marguerite Larrimer, I do not know the details of what happened to her. Charles Larrimer was an arrogant man. They were all arrogant, you know, being brought up that way, as masters. Oh yes, your father and grandfather as well, Clara. But I would not allow them to get away with it. I would not stand for such behavior and you will not find any of them participating in this business." She flicked the pamphlet. "You cannot defend this kind of behavior, Clara. How do you think they will behave if we make excuses for them? Honor—you must never countenance men to behave in a dishonorable way in the name of your honor. If we do not tell them they are wrong, who will?"

"I wish more people in the South would share your opinion, Mrs. Shea," Ida said then. "If they did, we might be able to stop these lynchings."

Mrs. Shea patted her hand again. "People do not admit they are wrong, child. You are right to go to the Northerners and foreigners. I can influence only my own house, you know. At my age I have no choice but to leave it to younger people like yourself to change the world." She turned to Clara. "You must do as you will, my dear, but you have the opportunity to live a life beyond what was possible for me. Do not waste it on defending a past that does not even belong to you. I know your mother has demanded your return to the gentle bosom of your family. But I say, don't do it. Stay here and make the most of your opportunities for education and do not reject your friend for not believing the myths you were brought up with."

Clara bent her head without answering and her grandmother sighed, shaking her head. "You must make up your own mind, my dear." With that she ended the topic by taking up a teapot and firmly pouring steaming liquid from its spout. Then she and my mother cooperated to steer the conversation to calmer waters and soon we were discussing sights of the Fair, as if the earlier argument had never taken place.

When we left the suite, Ida was unnaturally quiet as we waited for the elevator.

"I hope the outcome of this visit has been more pleasant than you anticipated, Miss Wells," my mother told her.

"Yes, ma'am. Very pleasant." She pulled a sheet of paper from her bag and she handed it to me. "I am sorry I delayed giving this to you, Miss Cabot. I received it this morning. It is from the detective."

I grabbed it and read eagerly. "Roland Johnson is Robert Jones? Roland Johnson. But where is he, Ida? When last I saw him he was playing the violin at the Haitian pavilion." Ida looked uncomfortable. I explained to my mother that Detective Whitbread located Bessie Jones in Philadelphia and she told him that the younger brother of the man who was lynched went to New York, and then Paris, to study violin and that he changed his name to Roland Johnson.

"He left some weeks ago to return to New York," Ida told me. "But surely this will throw enough doubt on the case for them to release Dr. Chapman."

"I don't know but I must take this to the doctor's lawyer immediately. I know his office. Please, return without me. I can take this to him and then get a later train. Oh, Ida, thank you. Thank you."

As soon as the elevator reached the ground I was off without further conversation. It was late afternoon and I was determined to find Mr. Leventhal before he left his office.

NINETEEN

At the office, I had to behave very rudely in order to finally gain admittance to the man but when I had, I thrust the letter into his hands.

"Do you see? Mr. Roland Johnson was at the Columbian Exposition. He was one of the waiters at the Music Hall the night we were there and I saw him exchange a look of recognition with Mr. Larrimer. Of course, I had no idea what it meant at the time, but Larrimer most surely led the mob that lynched his brother. He had far more reason to kill the man than Dr. Chapman."

The lawyer was very quiet.

"You can use it, though, can't you?" I pleaded. "It will help him, won't it?"

He frowned. But he stood up and took his hat from a table. "Come, Miss Cabot. We must consult my client. It will be up to him."

I followed as he strode quickly from the room. I had no doubt the doctor must see the relevance of this information but I was grateful for the opportunity to see him when he got the news, which could only lift some of his worries.

Mr. Leventhal engaged a cab and we were driven to Harrison Street Station where the doctor had been moved. The lawyer quickly got us into a small, bare interview room and shortly afterwards Dr. Chapman was led in. The guard left to stand outside the door and Mr. Leventhal handed the doctor the letter without explanation. We waited while he read it. Finally, he looked up.

"Mr. Leventhal, will you give us a few moments alone? Please."

With a nod, the lawyer left the room. Dr. Chapman sat down across from me at the scarred wooden table. He looked up from the letter.

"Surely it will help," I began, but he put a hand up to stop me.

"I cannot use it. No, please, hear me out. It is the death by lynching of William Jones that Marguerite Larrimer told me about that evening at the Music Hall." He looked down at the letter in his hand. "I did not know. I had never heard. You cannot understand.

"I told you I visited the Larrimers and found Marguerite trapped in an unhappy marriage. What I did not tell you was how she came to me that day. She begged me to take her away with me. She said seeing me again had reminded her of all her previous hopes and dreams and she could no longer stay there. What could I do? I could not take her, a married woman, away with me. She begged for my protection but I did not wish to take her away with me and I refused her. She became hysterical and I was even more determined to extract myself from the situation. I tried to tell her she should return to her father but she said he would never countenance her leaving her husband. I told her I was sorry but I could not be the one to whom she came. I reminded her of an aunt of hers who I felt surely would take her in. I offered to contact the lady and to arrange for transportation.

"She spurned my offer and ran from the place cursing me. I packed my things and left on the next train. I thought the best thing I could do would be to cut off the acquaintance. I did not know. It was only that night at the Music Hall that I heard from her what happened. Despite what she said to me, she returned home and prepared to flee to her aunt, but her husband found her packed bags and accused her of planning to run away with me. He was wild. He refused to let her go. He even hit her, then in his anger and embarrassment at what he had done, and what she had been about to do, he accused the young Negro servant of attacking her. And he had the man lynched."

"He was vicious. Surely his actions prove it. Surely this story proves there were others more likely to wish him dead?"

"What would you have me do? Accuse Robert Jones? Listen to me, Emily. The reason Marguerite told me the story that night was because Roland Johnson had contacted her. In a letter he begged for her to meet with him. The one thing he wanted was to clear his dead brother's name. He didn't want to kill Larrimer. He wanted her to write an account of the incident that would tell the truth of it. He just wanted to clear his brother's name.

"But she was terrified of her husband. He had already found a copy of the anti-lynching pamphlet and made a terrible scene. She feared worse but nonetheless she begged me to act on her behalf, to contact Roland Johnson to arrange a meeting. After failing her before, how could I deny that request? Nor did I want to. When I met you coming to the Haitian pavilion the next morning I had only just talked to Roland. He agreed to meet her that afternoon at the Dahomey Village. I found Marguerite and told her he would be there.

"How do you think I felt walking to tea with your brother only to learn they expected trouble on the Midway at the very place where I had arranged for them to meet? I rushed back to the dormitory and tried to telephone her. I was told she was sick with a headache. I called again and insisted it was an emergency. They tried to conceal it, but finally admitted she was gone. I raced to the Midway then and saw that man Weaver with a gang of thugs hanging around in the street as if waiting. I rushed into the exhibit asking for Marguerite. Just as someone pointed out the hut, there was a gunshot. I ran to the door and found Roland Johnson standing over Larrimer's body."

"Then he did shoot him."

"No more than I did." He looked at me wearily. "There was no gun in his hand and he was shaking with surprise and fear, telling me over and over that he did not do it. He said Larrimer had tried to shoot him but was struck down himself instead. He was hysterical. I sent him away."

"But why?"

"Don't you see? I did not kill the man and had no gun, yet see where it has gotten me. What do you think would have happened to Roland? And having been arrested, of the two of us, who do you think would get the fairer trial? Do you know what they would do to him?

"Don't you see, Emily, I couldn't do that. If I had taken Marguerite away as she begged me five years ago, William Jones would never have been lynched. Would you have me now be responsible for the hanging of his brother?"

"But we will help him. We will see to it he gets a fair trial," I insisted. But the doctor crumpled Whitbread's letter in his hand and shook his head.

"His defense would be no different than mine. I had no gun and someone else shot the man. If a trial will take place on that basis it is easy to see that I stand a much better chance of acquittal. In any case it is too late, don't you see? Even if I tried to say he was in the hut, there would be an assumption of guilt or conspiracy on my part as well, since I did not speak sooner. No, I will not permit it, Emily. I made that decision when you and your brother walked through the door of the hut that night. Testimony of Roland's presence would be useless."

I could see he would not back down. I had thought all would be resolved with this information. Detective Whitbread had risked, and probably lost, his job to get it but it was all for nothing. Dr. Chapman would be tried and probably found guilty. That unspoken fact stood between us.

He came around the table and leaned back against it. "I am greatly touched by your efforts to help me, Emily, but it is in vain. I can tell you, as a doctor, that there are many times when there is no treatment and no cure. In those cases you must stand back and let things take their course. So it is now—you must let things take their course. They may yet work out right. We do not know."

I was startled when the door opened and Mr. Leventhal returned to tell us our time was up. He saw the letter crumpled in the doctor's hand and a pained look crossed his face. I perceived he had already been informed by his client concerning Roland Johnson and was instructed not to use this information. Dr. Chapman bowed slightly after returning the letter to me and I allowed the lawyer to lead me out. He told me he was very sorry when he delivered me to the station for the train back to Hyde Park.

It was dark when I entered the Haitian pavilion to return the letter to Ida and to tell her and Mr. Barnett why it was useless to continue the investigation. Ida could not understand it.

"But didn't you explain to him that Roland Johnson has already left town and cannot be in danger of being arrested?"

"He will not have it come out. He says that Roland is as innocent as he is but would be less likely to get a fair trial."

Ida and Mr. Barnett exchanged a glance.

"I think he feels responsible for the death of William Jones."

Ida snorted. "Nonsense. He was not part of the lynch mob. He is a very stubborn man."

"Oh, he is. In any case, we must wire Detective Whitbread. If he has not already broken off his chase to return to deal with his own affairs, he must do so now. I am only worried that he will insist on finding Roland Johnson anyhow. It would be like him to want to interview him, even if he believed Roland innocent."

"Stubborn man," she said again, stamping her foot.

"Ida," Mr. Barnett said in a warning tone.

"No. We must show her. Come, Miss Cabot."

She hurried away and I followed, as she marched up the grand staircase, mumbling angrily to herself. Mr. Barnett followed with a sigh, shaking his head all the way.

Everyone else, it seemed, had left for the day and the rooms we passed were empty, although electric lights burned. At the end of a corridor she reached up and found a cord which pulled down an opening in the ceiling and provided a small ladder. I followed her up it to an attic where we found a makeshift bedroom. Roland Johnson jumped up from a cot. There was an oil lamp on a small table and the windows were shrouded with sheets.

"We hid him here, after the murder," Ida told me. "Roland, this is Miss Emily Cabot. She has come from Dr. Chapman who refuses to admit you were on the scene when Mr. Larrimer was murdered."

"Did you see who fired the shot?" I asked, breathless from climbing.

"Of course, he did not," Ida told me, "or we would have told you. Tell her what you did see, Roland."

The boy looked across at Barnett but the older man nodded wearily and he told his tale eagerly enough after that. When he and his sister fled Sherville, he kept his dead brother's violin as his only remembrance. He quickly took to the instrument with a passion that was recognized by a patron who sent him to New York, and later Paris, to study. It was his sister's idea for him to change his name as she lived in fear of Larrimer after what had happened. Roland's talent was fostered and he was encouraged by his teachers. When he was offered the opportunity to come to the Fair, he seized it.

Seeing the Larrimers had been entirely due to chance and fear had made him hide when he first recognized them. But he soon became obsessed with the idea of clearing his brother's name, so he followed them to their hotel and bribed a busboy to deliver a note and a copy of the pamphlet to Mrs. Larrimer. He had hoped to get her written statement regarding what had really happened, and that was his intention when Dr. Chapman arranged the meeting.

But, when he arrived at the Dahomey Village that night, he found not only Marguerite Larrimer but also her husband. Larrimer was in a fit of anger. He slapped his wife and called her a traitor. When Roland tried to protest, Larrimer pulled out the gun and Mrs. Larrimer escaped. The enraged husband was hitting the boy with a stick and telling him he would not get away and he would never be able to tell anyone about his brother. He claimed he had men outside who would cause a riot and no one would ever know how he had died. He was in tears cursing Roland for ever having appeared to dig up the past. In the middle of this rage a shot rang out and Larrimer fell to the floor. Roland was bending over him when Dr. Chapman appeared and the boy pleaded with him that he had not done the shooting. Larrimer had been prepared to shoot him. When Dr. Chapman told him to flee, he did so immediately, running back to the pavilion where he found Miss Wells and Mr. Barnett and told them all. Anxious for his safety, they hid him in the attic and there he remained.

"So you didn't see who shot him, then?" I asked.

"No, ma'am. But he said he had men outside and I believed him. He said he was going to shoot me so I couldn't ever tell anybody about anything."

Mr. Barnett snorted. "What an arrogant coward. He was going to shoot you, so no one would know how he had your brother lynched and then he was going to cover it up by a riot? Lord knows we have our troubles but he'd never have gotten away with that here."

"But there were men—outside the gates of the exhibit," I told them, remembering Weaver leaning against a wall. I shivered.

"They've got a rough crowd down there. Some of them would do anything for money. There's truth enough in that," Mr. Barnett told us. "But the local authorities wouldn't let them get away with it. Not if they knew."

I thought of Fitz. "But maybe they didn't know. It seems to me Mr. Fitzgibbons from the mayor's office may have had trouble keeping Larrimer in check. And he knew the gamblers. His father-in-law owed them money."

"Now you are talking. There are men on the Midway who would kill over gambling money without blinking. That I could believe."

"It must have been one of them but how to prove it?"

"You'd have to get one of his buddies to tell on him, I think."

"Well, in any case, you're out of danger, Roland. Dr. Chapman will never admit you were there."

Mr. Barnett shook his head. "He may be out of danger from the law, Miss Cabot, but you're forgetting the man who did the shooting. That's why he broke into my house. He was looking for Roland."

"But I thought it was to steal the accounts of the lynching at Sherville that it was done."

Mr. Barnett looked embarrassed. "No. He was looking for Roland. I hid those newspaper accounts of the Sherville incident. I was afraid they would lead you to Roland. But the effort was wasted when Ida insisted on pursuing the story anyhow." Ida glared at him, but Mr. Barnett continued. "I didn't see who it was that was looking for Roland that evening but whatever reason he had for killing Larrimer, an even better one would be to preserve his own skin."

"But Roland didn't see him," Ida protested.

"You think he knows that? You think he can take a chance on it? No, I think Roland had better stay right here until we can smuggle him back to New York or, even better, Paris."

I stared at Mr. Barnett. We could all agree it was best for Roland to stay hidden but his statements had given me an idea of how to find the killer. It would be a risky strategy but the doctor's situation was fast becoming desperate.

TWENTY

*H*ave some more cake, Mr. Hanover. I'm sorry my mother is not here today. She is helping Miss Wells at the Haitian pavilion." I looked across at my brother Alden. We had arranged for Ida to request my mother's assistance. We knew she would not approve of our plan. "Actually we have had some very good news. We have every reason to believe our friend, Dr. Chapman, will soon be released." Lies, all lies, God forgive me but Alden had insisted that we needed to convince Teddy that this was true. There were so few options left to do something to keep the doctor from going to trial.

"It was Detective Whitbread. He got the evidence that will get him off," Alden told him. Teddy watched him with big eyes while he munched on the lemon cake. "And, of course, once they hear what he found with the doctor's university connections and all, they'll have to let him go. But City Hall still wants the detective to find whoever did it. So, he'll be on the case when he gets back."

"He's coming back? Whitbread's coming back?" Teddy's face crumpled in a frown.

"You see, it turns out there was a young colored man, Roland Johnson, who was with Larrimer when he was shot," I explained. "The doctor only came afterwards."

Teddy gulped. "Did he see who shot him then?"

I looked at Alden. "No, he didn't actually. It was too dark," I told him. We had to be careful, for it all depended on getting Teddy's cooperation.

Alden stepped in. "So, one of those men outside must have done it—one of the roughs he was paying to make trouble. The thing is, Teddy, before he left, Whitbread was sure it was about the gambling tent. He thought Larrimer threatened to expose it. If he had complained to the authorities about it they would have had to shut it down."

"No, mate. He knew about it, sure. But he just paid up for the old guy and that was that."

"But there's no way to prove that, is there?" Alden saw Teddy glance at me then duck his head. "It's all right. Emily wouldn't tell anything. She knows. In fact she was the one who thought we should warn you." Teddy looked at me with alarm and I thought my brother was really going too far but I could say nothing without endangering our well-thought-out plan. "You see," Alden continued, "Whitbread is coming back and City Hall wants someone to blame. They are looking for someone."

"You mean to say, you think they'll go after Marco?"

"That's what we think."

"But he wasn't even there. It was Weaver and his mates. They were the ones outside that night the Southerner got killed. Larrimer hired them, see. I don't know what he was trying to hide but when he paid off the debts he wanted Marco to find him some men. So we hooked him up with Weaver and them others. It was his own idea. Marco wasn't even there. They can't say it was him."

"But Dr. Chapman didn't do it either and that did not keep them from arresting him," I reminded him.

"And he has the university people behind him. They've got pull, they have. We've got no pull," he protested. "But Fitz can't let this happen, he won't."

"Because you've been paying him to let you run the gambling tent? I know, Alden told me. But there's no way you can prove you bribed him, is there? And, if City Hall wants someone to blame for the murder, do you really think those bribes will protect you? Besides, Fitz suspected you had some arrangement with Larrimer, didn't he? And he forbade it."

"How do you know? But, yeah, he was mad as hell saying we'd better not help that Larrimer start any trouble. Fitz wouldn't stand for any trouble. They were going after getting more money like, to keep the Fair open and they wouldn't stand for any funny business. But then Larrimer said if he didn't get what he wanted, he'd complain about the tent and they'd have to do something, close it down. Marco was caught between 'em. But he didn't do it. He wasn't there that night even."

"Mr. Hanover, my brother and I have a plan. We think if you could get the men together in one place, say the gambling tent . . . I mean the men who would have been there that night . . . If you could get them there at one time, and if I could get Mr. Barnett to bring Roland, and if they thought that Roland had seen the man who did the shooting, well that man would leave when he heard they were coming, wouldn't he?"

Teddy Hanover looked at me as if I had sprouted horns all of a sudden. "No, miss . . . no, I think Marco and me had better be getting out of town, is what I think. I think I'd better be going."

Alden shook his head. "You can't do it, Teddy. You wouldn't get away with it. Look, Detective Whitbread will follow you. If you try to leave town he'll be sure you did it then. See how far he went already? Kentucky, Philadelphia. Why, I'll bet he would follow you all the way to England if you went there."

Poor Teddy groaned.

"Mr. Hanover, I am sure I can get Mr. Barnett to bring Roland Johnson to the tent . . . to pretend he saw who did the shooting."

"Who'll believe that then, miss?"

"When the man panics and leaves, we'll all know," Alden told him. "All the others who are there . . . not just us. He'll show his hand. He'll have to leave town and everybody will know. Whitbread will find him."

I felt sorry for the Londoner, who was shaking his head dolefully. We were taking advantage of his belief that everybody in the world had more influence than he did. He believed the university influence would help protect the doctor, while, in truth, even our letters of recommendation seemed unlikely to make any difference. He had no idea that Detective Whitbread himself was very likely going to lose his job. We were deceiving him. It was only too easy to use our own influence over the young man. But we needed to find out who it was who had fired that gunshot. It was the only way we could really get the doctor released. If we could force the guilty party to react, then we would know who the culprit was, even if he wouldn't admit it and we couldn't prove it. But there would be only one chance. As soon as Roland Johnson faced the man without recognition the play would be over and the opportunity gone. The man had only to sit still to survive. The trick we were planning would not work more than once.

TWENTY-ONE

*T*he next evening we executed my plan. But there was one part of it that Teddy was not privy to.

"Emily, this is not going to work. I'll take you back to the entrance and you can go home. I'm telling you, it won't work."

"Oh, yes it will. And I am not leaving. Either you get me into that peek hole or I will sneak into the tent anyhow, Alden. I will not go home and leave it to you to do this alone. It may be that the man betrays himself by some slight act or word. You might miss it."

Alden was having serious doubts about a part of the plan I had insisted on. In describing the gambling tent to me, he had told me about a secret hiding place that was used to oversee the hands of others in card games. A little hidden cul-de-sac had been built into the tent. I immediately insisted that I should be placed there to witness the scene. My brother objected, but I was the older sibling and invoked that power over him. When we were younger, there were times when I dressed in his clothes to accomplish some deed disguised as a boy. On that night, I decided to repeat this behavior and, to his disgust, I donned pants and a jacket and hid my hair under a cap of his. We snuck into the Wild West Show where the gambling tent had been located for the night. It was frequently moved around the Midway to confuse the authorities.

We were hidden behind some barrels across from the opening but now we saw Marcos leave and with a final shrug, my brother grabbed my hand and pulled me across and into the darkness of the tent. A small table and a couple of wooden chairs filled the space. Alden quickly led me to a hidden flap in one corner of the room. Inside there was a musty smell of mildewed canvas. He showed me how to peek through a hidden slit to see the table.

"They use it to keep an eye on the rowdies," he said, picking up some scraps from the floor. "So, you must be very quiet and don't say a word, no matter what happens, see?"

"I promise."

"All right, then. I'll tuck you in. It'll be some time before anyone comes in."

With a final disapproving shake of his head, he closed the flap and I sat in darkness for a long time. It must have been a couple of hours before anyone arrived. It was enough time for me to regret I had insisted on being present. Eventually there was movement and talking and clinking of glasses. A cautious peek showed me a card game had begun and now I began to listen in earnest. There was a considerable amount of cursing interspersed in the conversations.

At last, Alden and Teddy came in with the man Weaver and a number of other rough looking characters. I couldn't be sure if I recognized them from the Midway the night of Mr. Larrimer's murder. I knew the evening had finally begun when I saw through my slit that Mr. Prendergast had arrived and was counting a wad of bills Marco had given him. This must be the bribe regularly paid to city officials to allow the gambling to go unnoticed. But I was not interested in bribes they might be paying. I only wanted to know who had fired the shot that killed Larrimer and it seemed they would not raise that issue until the preliminaries with the city representative had been completed.

It was Teddy who brought up the topic. "Say, mates. I want to warn you. My friend Alden, here, says we're to have some uninvited visitors tonight. Tell 'em." He pushed Alden forward.

"It's true. I told Teddy this afternoon. My sister is concerned with the doctor's defense. She says they found a young Negro who was there when Larrimer was killed. They think he saw the man who did it."

"Is that right?" Teddy was behind the bar pouring a drink. "So, who was it then?"

"Well, that's the thing you see. He doesn't know the man's name but he said he would know him if he saw him. You were there that night, weren't you, Weaver? Did you see who did it?"

Weaver lounged against the bar. He looked across at Alden from under the brim of his black hat and I had the terrible feeling he was looking at me. I ducked back from my view but realized immediately that it was only Alden he was seeing. He raked my brother up and down with a glance, then responded. "I was there all right. So were Jake, and Billy, and Tree. But we were outside the gate. Couldn't see a thing from there."

"Why were you there that night anyhow? I saw you all when I was going in." Alden asked him boldly. My brother and I both thought Weaver must have fired the shot, or, if he hadn't done it himself, he must know who had. But Teddy had disagreed on that point. I tried to see the expression on Weaver's face but he had his hat pulled down low over his eyes, as he always did, making it difficult to see his face.

One of the others started to laugh. "That was a good one. That rich guy wanted a bit of a ruckus. Paid for it, didn't he? So we showed up for the party but he done got shot in the back before it ever started. We got the dough for nothin'." He slapped his knee. "As good a night's work as I ever didn't do, I say. God rest his soul so long as I can keep his money. Wish there were a dozen more like him out there."

"Shut up," Weaver told him and the man turned back to hunch over his drink. Alden continued to face Weaver who was twirling a glass in his hand. He shrugged. There was a rumble from the other men. "Ten dollars," one of them added, "apiece." But they got quiet, waiting for Weaver to continue.

"Like the man says, ruckus never started. We were all outside. Right boys?" There was another rumble of agreement. "He never came out. Sent Hanover in for him."

This was a surprise, since Teddy had never mentioned this fact to us. Alden turned to him with a frown and Teddy looked harassed as he stepped out from behind the bar. "Sure. I ducked inside but didn't see nothing. Heard the shot and figured the deal was off. Wasn't supposed to be gunplay in the plans, was there then?"

Weaver stared at him.

Alden turned back to the tall man. "Are you trying to say Teddy had something to do with it? Why should he?"

Weaver smiled, his eyes still shadowed by the hat. "Guess he didn't mention Fitzgibbons, did he?"

Alden turned back to Teddy and I saw the barker shoot a gaze across at Marco but the older man refused to look at him. He had his head down pouring another drink. Teddy faced my brother. "Fitz found out Larrimer wanted to start something. I don't know how he found out about it, but he was furious about Larrimer's plan. He told Marco to call it off, that's all."

"Then, why didn't you?" Alden asked.

When Teddy looked away and didn't answer Weaver grunted. " 'Cause Larrimer threatened to tell the newspapermen Marco was paying off the city to let them run the game." He reached out a long finger to tap the wad of bills Prendergast was still counting. The city man froze. "Poor ol' Marco was in a pretty fix. If he let Larrimer have his fun, Fitz would shut down the game. If he didn't, Larrimer would make sure it was ruined. Nice it all worked out for you in the end, Marco."

"We didn't do nothing," Teddy rushed on, "We couldn't do nothing. Larrimer got shot before I ever found him. Anyhow, Mr. Prendergast here was in there longer than any of us that night."

"Hmm . . ." said Weaver as he turned to face the tall skinny man who stood beside the bar. "Mr. Prendergast. What were you doing there? Collecting for your masters?" His eyes dropped to the wad of bills and Prendergast stuffed them into a pocket. The room was silent.

"Well, I came to warn you, Marco," Alden continued when it was clear that the mayor's man had nothing to say. "My sister had the daft idea to have Barnett bring the boy, Roland, here to see if he could pick out the man."

There was another moment of silence then Marco spoke up. "Not here. He won't be allowed in here."

At that moment a man stumbled through the tent door, his eyes bulging. "Did you see that?" he asked, staring back out behind him.

"What's up your ass, Kiley? Come in and sit down if you're here to play," one of the others told him.

He turned back to his audience in the room. "Come, look. There's a whole crowd of darkies out there just standin' round with shovels and rakes. What's it for?"

Several of them rushed to his side to peer out and they confirmed his story. Weaver poured himself another drink then slouched back against the bar. "That there must be Mr. Barnett coming to unmask the shooter." He gulped down the contents of the glass. "Why Mr. Prendergast, where do you think you're going?" He stopped the man with his cold glare.

Then Alden raced across the room to confront the city man, putting himself between Prendergast and the tent flap. "Why, Mr. Prendergast, won't you stay to meet Mr. Johnson? Or are you afraid he'll recognize you?"

At that, I heard chairs scrape the floor as men moved away towards the walls and I saw Prendergast pull out a long barreled pistol and point it at my brother. Alden jumped back but froze when the gun was cocked. Weaver leaned forward to speak in Prendergast's ear. "Oh, so it was you, was it? Fitzgibbons found out Larrimer had hired men and was planning trouble. Did you tell him? Followed the man around for your boss, didn't you? Like a dog. A huntin' dog. You heard Larrimer say he was gonna start something. You told Fitzgibbons. What did Fitz tell you? Not to let it happen? I know. I bet he said you'd finally get that corporation counsel job, didn't he? If you just kept Larrimer from starting trouble."

Prendergast was shaking. Weaver turned to sip his drink with his back propped against the bar again. I couldn't understand how he could be so calm. I was mesmerized by the gun Prendergast still pointed at my brother. I wanted to tell Alden to keep quiet and get out of his way.

Then Alden opened his mouth. "Of course. No wonder you were on the scene so quickly. You were assigned to follow Larrimer. You were watching. You saw him slap around Mrs. Larrimer but you didn't stop him for that. It was only when you saw him going for Roland. He was going to shoot him and cover it by a riot. You couldn't let that happen. Fitz had told you to stop him."

The gun went off with a loud crash and a cloud of acrid smoke. I screamed and tore my way out of the hideaway. The men all looked at me with amazement. I saw Alden getting up from the floor dusting off his knees. He was all right, thank God. He must have jumped out of the way.

But now Prendergast stood across from me with the gun pointed at my head. His hand was shaking slightly. I couldn't take my eyes from the hole at the end of that gun but I heard Teddy yell "No!" I was aware of Weaver's smiling face beside that of Prendergast as it hung above the gun. Everyone else had frozen in silent tension.

Only Weaver dared to speak, "Poor Mr. Prendergast. If they didn't give you the corporation counsel job for doing that, they'll never give it to you now, will they? Not after everybody knows about it. Tut, tut, no siree. Can't have no murderer in the counsel's office."

Prendergast fired again and I fell to the floor on my back, a heavy weight on top of me. Prendergast edged out of the door, all the while pointing the gun so that the men stood still with their hands raised. Through the open flap of the door I could see Barnett's men part to let Prendergast through. Then he disappeared into the night.

There was a moan. I felt wetness and looked at blood on my hand but realized it wasn't my own. Teddy lay over me, shot. Alden rushed to me and helped turn him over. He lay in my arms as Alden yelled for someone to go fetch a doctor and men ran from the door. Teddy winced in pain and I heard Weaver's voice. "Too late for a doctor. They're just getting their tails out of here before the cops come and I guess this is where I follow suit."

I glared at him but he just smiled and walked out as if nothing had happened.

Alden latched on to one man, making him promise to go for help, and Marco came over with towels and a bottle. He tried to stop the bleeding while I sat there helplessly with Teddy's weight holding me down. I put my arm under his head.

Teddy groaned. "He got me final, I think."

"No, don't say that," I protested uselessly.

"No." Alden dropped down to his side. "Hold on. I sent for help. My God, Emily, you would have been dead but for Teddy."

That actually made the injured man smile. My eyes swam with tears while Marco cursed and took a drink from his bottle.

"Anyhow, we got him," Alden said. He glanced at me to warn there was little hope. "It was Prendergast."

"Yes. And now everyone will know." I pressed on the towels which were getting soaked with blood and sobbed. Everyone would know he had killed Teddy as well. That was only too clear now. I felt an icy pain up my spine. Oh, no. This couldn't be happening. Only a moment before Teddy had been whole but now he was leaking all over his ugly green and red plaid suit. The blood wouldn't stop pooling out, staining the fibers. He would never get it out of the wool. Oh, no. I grasped at the towels trying to press them to his chest, trying to get it to stop.

Teddy frowned. "No. They won't believe it."

"Of course they will," I insisted, coughing the words on the verge of a sob. "He admitted it, didn't he? And we were all witnesses. Or, at least, why else would he have fired the gun like that?"

"Won't do no good." He was having trouble breathing. His air came out like a wheeze. "Ain't no one going to believe in what's sworn to by a bunch of gamblers, even if they would swear like. He's protected, see? I'm sorry, miss, they won't believe it."

"Oh, Teddy, don't worry about that. The law will get him. I promise you." That icy knife was still cutting into my back. "Oh, Teddy, I am so sorry you were the one to get hurt. I never should have jumped out like that. Please, be all right. I am so sorry."

His face lit up a bit. "That's OK, miss." He closed his eyes and struggled to speak. "You and your brother have been good to me." He was weakening and Alden put his hands to his face. "Couldn't let him shoot you, miss."

I sat there some time longer until he finally slipped away. Marco held his hand, weeping as he drank from the bottle. I cradled his head and brushed back the thatch of hair. There was nothing I could do. It had been my foolish idea to insist on being present. It had been my foolish act to jump out like that and draw Prendergast's fire. It should have been me lying there with life slipping away. The terrible weight of consequences held me down more firmly than the weight of Teddy Hanover's body on my legs. He was destroyed forever, as surely as a glass would, if it were dropped in carelessness and shattered at my feet.

It was done, and there was nothing I could ever do to recall it. I sobbed against the heavy weight on my chest. I sat there rocking uselessly until he grew cold and Alden was the one who got someone to look after Marco and helped me up, insisting I sit on a chair to wait for the police.

TWENTY-TWO

*T*eddy had been so right when he told me with his dying breath that Prendergast would not be convicted on the basis of what we had heard in the gambling tent or even the shooting we had witnessed. By the time police arrived that night, the men had faded away into the darkness. Even Marco had been led away. When Alden and I told our story again and again, we found ourselves charged with gaming and it was only in deference to my sex that they let me go. When I returned with bail for Alden the next morning, after a sleepless night, I insisted on knowing whether Prendergast had been arrested. The detective looked pained.

"You must have been mistaken, miss. He was with Mr. Fitzgibbons and some of the others on the mayor's staff, so he couldn't have been there."

"But that is a lie. He was there, in the tent, collecting a bribe for the city. That's why they're saying he was with them. We saw him shoot Teddy Hanover dead. Did you even look for the other men?"

"Of course we did. They say they weren't there. What do you expect? It was an illegal gambling den by your own account. And why should we believe you, missy?" He began to get irritated. "How do we know you're telling the truth? And if what you say is true, what was a woman doing there unless you were up to no good? Get on with you, and be grateful your brother's fine isn't more, or I'll arrest you on suspicion of prostitution."

"Prostitution? How dare you?"

But Alden was tugging on my arm and I knew it was useless to argue.

When we returned home there was a summons from my department chair, Mr. Small. It required my immediate attention and was phrased in such a way that I could not ignore it. Accompanied by a smug Mr. Lukas and a sorry Mr. Reed, Mr. Small met me in a classroom of Cobb Hall. In the course of the proceedings I had to admit that I had been absent from my work and classes in the last week. The interrogation seemed pointless. What did it matter?

Mr. Small addressed me from behind the desk. "This would be a serious concern, Miss Cabot, but another matter has been brought to our attention that is so grave as to make your lack of diligence a minor point. We have learned that you were present last night at a gambling hall where a shooting took place. Is this true?"

I glanced at Lukas and saw a grim smile. I had no doubt Weaver had told him of my presence.

"Yes. I was there, but there was a reason for my presence, a very good reason."

"Miss Cabot, surely you are aware that the rules of the university absolutely forbid students to frequent such places. It is grounds for immediate expulsion." He waved a hand when I tried to speak. "Please, let me continue. This incident was brought to President Harper's attention this morning when a representative of the city lodged a complaint concerning your presence. It was the topic of heated debate at the University Council meeting. The result, I am most sorry to say, is that you are hereby suspended from the university. It is difficult to understand how you could commit so blatant an offense. Surely you know how careful we have been to avoid the sensationalism of the press. It was only because President Harper assured the man that you would be disciplined, that your name and affiliation with the university were suppressed from the newspaper accounts. Miss Talbot and Mr.

Reed spoke fervently in your defense but even they had to agree that this could not be overlooked. Your dismissal need not be final but you will have to reapply after a decent period. I am sorry to be the one to have to tell you this, but you must see that there could be no other result based on your actions."

"Mr. Small, please, a great injustice is being done. The reason I was present last night, with my brother, was to expose the man who murdered Mr. Charles Larrimer. Stephen Chapman is imprisoned wrongly for that deed. In the course of the night we learned that a man named Prendergast who works for the mayor actually shot Larrimer. Last night he shot Teddy Hanover, a young man who worked on the Midway. He shot him before our eyes but the police will not believe it. You must help us to right this terrible wrong, or Dr. Chapman will be condemned to death for something he did not do. Cannot you or President Harper help us to prove the truth of this matter?"

I saw him exchange a glance with Professor Lukas, then Lukas spoke. "This is nonsense. She is raving. If you associate with the type of men who frequent gambling dens, Miss Cabot, you will witness violence like this shooting. As for your claims that somehow the true murderer of Mr. Larrimer was revealed on this occasion, how do you expect us to credit such a claim? Do you think these men are to be believed? This is what happens when you insist on frequenting such a place. Men like that will say anything, do anything."

He stood there so tall and smug. Who was he to condemn the likes of Teddy Hanover? I protested, "Mr. Weaver is a man I have seen much in your company, Professor. He was there last night. I have no doubt he told you all about it." I turned to Professor Small. "How is it that it is all right for Mr. Lukas to associate with the likes of Weaver while I am to be condemned for trying to prove Dr. Chapman's innocence?"

Mr. Small stood up from the desk. "It is not Professor Lukas's conduct that is in question here, Miss Cabot. It is your own. There is no possible justification for your going to such a place. That is final."

"But Prendergast shot Charles Larrimer—and he shot Teddy Hanover before my very eyes— yet the police refuse to arrest him."

"Miss Cabot, if you have information about either of these crimes, you must give it to the local authorities and they have the responsibility for pursuing the investigation. It is not for you to say. Dr. Chapman has been provided with an attorney. We must allow him to conduct the doctor's case. We cannot usurp the roles of appointed and elected court officials. By your own account it is your attempt to do so that has led to the unfortunate events of yesterday evening."

That stung me. It was only too true. "I see. You will not help then. And I am expelled. I understand. You will have to excuse me, Mr. Small, Mr. Reed. I must prepare to attend a funeral for the young man who died last night. A death for which no one will be made to pay." I swept from the room, unwilling to listen to any more.

I ran down three flights of stairs and out the front but as I started down Fifty-seventh Street, I began to dread returning to my mother with this news. I saw a stand of trees and took refuge in it, dropping to the ground behind a large trunk. Ignoring the damp pile of leaves beneath me, I sank to the ground and put my head in my hands. What had I done? Teddy was dead and no one would believe that Prendergast had shot him or that Prendergast had shot Charles Larrimer. I saw before my eyes a courtroom, full to the brim with people and reporters, where Dr. Chapman would face a trial without hope of the truth coming out. They would never force Prendergast to admit he had shot Larrimer and they would never arrest him. No hint of a connection to City Hall would be allowed and Stephen Chapman would be condemned. As surely as I would never see Teddy Hanover again—after he was buried in the earth the next day—I would never again see Stephen Chapman.

Certainly they would never listen to me, a discredited woman student who had been expelled from the university. What a mess I had made of things. I so wished my father was with me. I knew he would have been able to deal with these circumstances. He would have been terribly disappointed in me, though. What had I thought to accomplish by going to that gambling tent? If I had not done so, Teddy would still be alive and perhaps there would be a way to prove Prendergast had killed Larrimer. It came to me that I could never take back what I had done. I could never undo it. Teddy was gone, gone, gone and Stephen was sure to follow. My vision clouded over and I dug my fingers into my scalp. Finally, I realized I could not sit in the cold and damp forever, so I stood and brushing away slick brown leaves that clung to my skirt, I trudged back to our lodgings.

My mother tried to comfort me when I told her the news. Dean Talbot had visited her in my absence and now she understood the seriousness of the situation. The Dean wished to see me, but I could not face the interview, so I put it off. I knew she would have some scheme or plan to salvage my career at the university but I could not see myself returning to my compilations of statistics while Dr. Chapman was hanged for a crime he did not commit. I had come to the university with a clear course, and had held to it steadily, despite the opposition of Professor Lukas, but now I had lost my way and like a rudderless boat bobbed helplessly on the waves of this storm. Everything I had tried to do had failed and there was nothing left to hold on to.

TWENTY-THREE

*T*he following day was one of the last for the Exposition. Huge crowds were expected and the mayors of cities around the country had come to hear Carter Harrison make a final plea for the monies to reopen the Fair in the spring.

But we were a smaller and sadder group that gathered at Teddy's grave in the paupers' cemetery to say a final goodbye. My mother arranged for a clergyman and rented a carriage for ourselves and Mr. Marco. That man was deeply grieved and he staggered a bit at the graveside, making it obvious that he had been drinking. But my mother took his arm gently and provided balance during the brief ceremony. He refused to join us for tea when we returned but spoke briefly to Alden and staggered off.

"Are you quite sure Mr. Marco will be all right?" my mother asked as we removed our hats and coats.

Alden stood there, hands in the pockets of his overcoat. "I'm not, actually. He said he was going to the Fair to look up his old friend, Fitz. He is quite overcome by Teddy's death, you know."

"Fitz!" I said. "He will be with the mayor. Surely Prendergast will not be with them. Will he?" Alden looked worried. "You don't think Mr. Marco intends to attack him?"

"He's not in his right mind. And you could see he's been drinking."

I started to put my coat back on. "We had better go after him."

Alden watched me uneasily. "I'll go. You'd better not come, Em. You've had enough trouble as it is."

"So much so that more doesn't matter, I think. It was my fault, Alden. It was my stupid plan that got Teddy killed. Come on."

My mother watched in resigned silence as I rushed from the house and Alden followed. We stopped at the Ferris Wheel and were told Marco had been there and left. Alden mumbled that he probably took a gun as we hurried through the crowds of the Midway to the grounds of the Fair. Paying the entrance fee, Alden got hold of a flyer that said the activities for the day were at the Music Hall. We came to large crowds as we neared that building and Alden jumped up on to a balustrade, scanning the crowds for Marco.

"I see him." Alden jumped down again. "He went into the building. Come on."

Inside the Music Hall Mayor Carter Harrison was addressing an audience of mayors and city officials from across the country. With a facility I could never understand, Alden got us past a guard on the door and we tiptoed inside where Harrison was speaking.

The mayor's voice boomed out in the high ceilinged room. "It almost sickens me, when I look at this great Exposition, to think that it will be allowed to crumble to dust. In a few days the building wrecker will take hold of it and it will be torn down, and all of this wonderful beauty will be scattered to the winds of heaven."

We looked around frantically, trying to spot Marco. I nudged Alden and pointed when I saw Fitz and Prendergast on a side of the hall near the front. Alden grabbed my hand and started leading me through the crowd of standing men on that side. Harrison's voice held their attention.

"Mr. Burnham, the architect and partner of Mr. Root, who is really the designer of this thing . . . poor Root, is dead, gone forever, but it is a pleasing thought that perhaps he may look down and see what has been done. It must be a feeling of great pleasure and great pride when he looks down on what he has designed. Mr. Burnham said the other day, 'Let it go. It has to go, so let it go. Let us put the torch to it and burn it down.'"

We were stuck in the throng, which had gotten thicker. Alden jumped up to the ledge of a column and, hugging it, peered towards where Prendergast was standing. Around us the audience was too mesmerized by the mayor to notice.

"Come on," Alden whispered in my ear. He jumped down and slid along the wall, pulling me after him while the speech continued.

"I believe with him," Harrison declaimed. "If we cannot preserve it for another year, I would be in favor of putting a torch to it and burning it down and letting it go up into the bright sky to eternal heaven."

Alden pulled me through an opening into one of the side rooms like the one where Larrimer had held his dinner party. As I looked back, I saw Fitz turn his head and frown when he recognized us. Prendergast stood beside him like a statue.

I coughed at smoke from inside the room and saw Alden push Marco away from a small pile of papers that had been set on fire under a wooden table. It seemed Marco had been inspired by the mayor's words and tried to begin the final conflagration. Luckily it was an inefficient attempt and even though he had poured whiskey from his bottle to help it along, Alden and I were able to stamp it out quickly.

But the small amount of smoke had drawn men from the main room, led by Fitz with Prendergast behind him. Marco spun around to face them, teary eyed, with a pistol in his hand.

Fitz held the others back but he hissed, "Open those windows."

With a wary eye on Marco's gun, one of the men obeyed.

"No, Marco," Alden whispered. "This isn't the way."

"He killed Teddy." Marco waved the gun, and some of the men retreated, but Fitz stood still.

"Put it down, Marco."

"Let it go," Alden said gently. "Let it go, Marco." And, as the drunken man watched him with bleary eyes, my brother walked calmly over and put his hand on the gun.

"Let them all burn," Marco mumbled and as soon as he let his hand drop to his side men fell on him but he hardly struggled.

"Be quiet," Fitz hissed, and he silently directed the policemen who had been summoned. They surrounded Marco and rushed him away.

When Alden made to follow, Fitz caught him by the arm. "What do you think you are doing?"

I stepped up to them. "He was stopping him. Prendergast shot Teddy Hanover Thursday night. Alden and I were there. We saw him." I was glaring at the tall thin man and Fitz turned to glare at him, too.

"Get out of here," he ordered, and with a last angry look Prendergast turned and ran away.

"Stop him. He's getting away," I said. But Fitz had a firm grip on my elbow.

"Not here. Come with me, both of you."

I exchanged a glance with Alden and we followed the Irishman out of the hall where applause was greeting the end of the mayor's speech. Fitz fought his way through the crowds to a door where he ordered a carriage and ushered us into it.

As we headed for the city we told him all that had happened and demanded he arrest Prendergast for the murders of Larrimer and Teddy. He listened warily and I was sure he was already aware of the facts. We wore ourselves out with arguments until we finally reached City Hall where he led us into his office and closed the door.

There he left us for some time, saying he would have to get the police to give him a full account. An hour later he began a parade of police detectives and officials reporting to him on the case. We protested the lies they reported concerning the alibi of Mr. Prendergast and the claims by those who had been in the tent that they were elsewhere. I was most infuriated by the officer who had threatened to charge me with prostitution asserting blandly that he had done no such thing.

Several times during these exchanges, Fitz's secretary attempted to interrupt but was waved away. When Fitz was at last wearing us down to an admission that there was nothing to be done in the face of such testimony, he finally listened to what the man was trying to tell him.

"It was Mr. Prendergast, sir. He tried several times to see you."

Alden groaned and Fitz frowned.

"He's gone now. But I thought you would not be pleased that he threatened to petition the mayor himself. I told him I was sure you wouldn't approve. He was on with his thing again, sir. You know . . . about the corporation counsel."

Fitz rolled his eyes. "Corporation counsel. He's wise if he stays out of sight to keep himself out of jail, the fool. At least he won't be able to bother Harrison. The mayor is tied up all day with the visitors."

"No, sir," said his secretary, consulting a notebook. "He'll be home now. The festivities were over a couple of hours ago and he has nothing this evening. You know how anyone is welcome to petition Mayor Harrison. His door is always open. I believe it was the intention of Mr. Prendergast to complain once again to the mayor's face as he has tried many times before. He was very insistent."

Fitz stood, a look of horror on his face. "He didn't go to the house?"

"I don't know, sir, but I thought he might."

Fitz pushed the man out of his way and rushed out calling for his carriage. Without a moment's hesitation Alden and I followed and he did not object when we joined him.

"He can't mean anything by it. He won't have gone there—I forbade it. I told him he'd have nothing at all if he tried that again."

Alden shook his head. "He shot Teddy point blank, Fitz. He's a madman."

Fitz shouted at the driver to hurry and in a few minutes we were in front of the mayor's house. Fitz jumped down and Alden was helping me out when we heard the explosive sound of a shot.

"No," Fitz yelled, running for the door.

It was opened by Prendergast who ran by us.

"Stop!" Alden attempted to grab him but he flung my brother to the ground and disappeared. Meanwhile Fitz had already entered the house and I followed him into a study where he stood back in shock.

Mayor Harrison lay on the floor. Two other men bent over him. I recognized a young man in a dressing gown as the mayor's son. The other man was older and he was arguing with the injured mayor telling him he wasn't dying.

"I'm dying, you fool. I'm dying."

There was not much blood on his chest but I could see a pool of it spreading out from beneath him. I glanced at Fitz but he stood there stunned into silence. The mayor's son was on the telephone calling for help but before the ambulance and police arrived he was gone. As the family wept, and officials began to arrive, I followed Fitz out to the front where we found Alden struggling in the arms of a policeman.

"Prendergast. It was Prendergast. I tried to catch him but he got away. Fitz, tell them."

Fitz nodded and two patrolmen rushed away in the direction that Prendergast had disappeared. As more men arrived Alden and I watched Fitz wander onto the lawn, looking up at the night sky and keening. It was a horrible sound from such an unexpected source. My brother put an arm around my shoulders and pulled me close.

TWENTY-FOUR

*I*t was on the day of Carter Harrison's funeral that we were finally able to confront Fitz again. Prendergast had surrendered to police barely an hour after he shot the mayor. He had been charged with that murder but nothing had been done about the deaths of Larrimer and Teddy. Dr. Chapman was still in jail and I despaired of ever having the truth revealed. No one would listen to us and we were regarded with suspicion. I no longer could even claim the respectability of an association with a university that had expelled me.

But Detective Whitbread had returned and, on making a full report to Miss Wells and Mr. Barnett, he learned of the new developments. It was at his insistence that Fitz grudgingly granted an interview in his office following the mayor's funeral. It was a white-faced Mr. Fitzgibbons, surrounded by packing boxes, who faced Detective Whitbread, Miss Wells, Mr. Barnett, my brother and me. It was late afternoon, after the huge procession, through a city thronged with crowds, had seen Carter Harrison to his final rest.

"I don't know what you expect of me," he said nodding at the boxes. "As you can see, my place here is ending with the change of administration."

"Prendergast must be charged with the murders of Charles Larrimer and Theodore Hanover," Detective Whitbread stated our demands. "And Stephen Chapman must be released and declared innocent of all charges."

"And what good would that do?" Fitz asked. "Prendergast will be convicted of the murder of the mayor and, unless they get him off on a plea of insanity, which he will never agree to—he thinks he's right as rain, the daft bugger—he will hang. What good would it do to cloud the issue by accusing him of two deaths where his guilt can't be proved? No one will believe a bunch of thugs from a gambling den. You know that, Whitey. They aren't good witnesses even if they would testify, which they won't. What good would it do to even charge him?"

"It would be justice," Ida Wells told him. "It would be the truth."

"I'm sorry, miss, but no one is going to charge Prendergast with those murders. He will hang for killing Carter Harrison and that is all the justice that's wanted."

Justice. That was his idea of justice? I was cold with anger. "Besides," I said, "who would want to expose the reasons behind the earlier killings? Who would want it known that Larrimer was a threat to the city administration and that was the reason he had to die? He was going to cause a riot, he was going to shoot Roland Johnson, and cover his act by creating a disturbance. But the city wouldn't have that. It would endanger the attempt to keep the Fair open another year, wouldn't it? And how would it make you look? You were assigned to keep the Southerner in line and you set Prendergast to watch him. But when he became a threat he had to go, and the unstable Prendergast stopped him on your orders." I shook my head. "Oh, I'm sure you didn't tell him to shoot the man but you knew his obsession with the corporation counsel job, didn't you? Did you promise him that job, for which he had no qualifications and which you never intended to give him? You fooled him . . . you promised it on the condition he stop Larrimer. Then when he executed your command you told him he could never have the position because of what he had done. And that was what led him to shoot Harrison in the end, wasn't it? How responsible do you feel for that?"

There were tears in Fitz's eyes and he brushed them away. "There's nothing I can do, woman. Can't you see I'm on my way out of here?"

Barnett glanced around at the boxes. "But what if it came out? Do you want that? Do even the new inhabitants of these offices want it to come out?" He eyed the city man coolly. "I'm here to tell you that unless you drop the charges against Dr. Chapman and charge Prendergast instead, I am prepared to print a series of articles unveiling the truth, not only about Prendergast's relationship with Larrimer, but his presence and errand at the gambling tent. How would you like to see it described in print how the gamblers paid a bribe to City Hall to stay in business and how Prendergast appeared every week to collect it?"

"No one would believe you."

"Perhaps not, and you are thinking the circulation of the *Conservator* is confined to the Negro community. True. But how long do you think it will be before the other papers pick it up? You may be too loyal to the memory of your late mayor to want to tarnish his name but you know he had many enemies, most of them powerful."

"You would do that to Harrison even after he's dead?" Fitz was furious.

"You would have Dr. Chapman hang just to keep the mayor's memory bright?" Detective Whitbread responded.

Fitz threw down a pen he had been fingering. "I think I can get Chapman released but there is no way anyone will be willing to charge Prendergast with the other murders."

"But the doctor's reputation will never be completely cleared if the truth is not revealed," I protested.

Fitz shrugged, "He'll have his neck. But you can never print it."

Mr. Barnett looked at me and I nodded. He turned back to Fitz. "You have until tomorrow. I see no point in sullying Harrison's memory but we won't let you sacrifice the doctor."

As we filed from the room I took a final look at Fitz carefully packing away his photographs and I wondered what would become of him.

TWENTY-FIVE

*M*ust you really go, Ida?" I asked.

"My friends in England have arranged for my passage," she told me, as she handed down more volumes from the shelves. "It is a sad fact that I can more easily get a hearing in that country than here in the land of the free and the home of the brave."

We were helping to pack up Mr. Douglass's books and papers in his study of the Haitian pavilion. Outside it was dark, as rain drummed on the roof and windows. It was several days after we had met with Mr. Fitzgibbons. Dr. Chapman had been released but it had been deemed prudent to send Alden to meet him and I was somewhat disappointed when my brother returned without the doctor. The released man had gone to meet with Marguerite Larrimer at her hotel in response to an urgent entreaty. I was aware that she had returned to Chicago for the trial but what her business was with the doctor now that he was free, my brother could not say. I had not yet seen Dr. Chapman when my mother brought me to help with the final packing at the pavilion.

"Surely your friends here must want you to stay?"

Ida climbed down the little ladder and helped me to tie up the box.

"It is true, there are those who would not have me go. Mr. Barnett has made a proposal."

"A proposal? Marriage, you mean? But that is wonderful, Ida."

"I have told him I would consider it, but first I must at least attempt to achieve some justice for those who have died," she said, pulling over another box and beginning to fill it.

"But will he wait?"

"We shall see. Perhaps he will grow tired."

"Oh, Ida, I hope you will return and marry Mr. Barnett. At least then something would be salvaged from all this."

At that moment we heard the notes from a violin. It was the theme from *Scheherazade* again.

"And what of Roland?"

"He comes with me to New York and will sail on the same ship to England. From there he will go on to Paris to continue his studies."

"So you will both go to Europe." I sat down on one of the packed boxes.

"And what of you, Miss Cabot? What will you do?"

No matter how many times I entreated Ida to call me by my first name, she always reverted to the more formal address. There was a wariness in her attitude that I feared would never be completely dispelled.

"I don't know. I am expelled from the university. I'll never get the fellowship back. I should return to Boston with my mother but she encourages me to stay. She says 'something will turn up.' I know she wants me to continue my studies but it is impossible." I stood and began to pace. "My brother, Alden, announced that he will stay. He is being completely unreasonable. He should return to his position at my uncle's bank, he has been gone a month. We have argued about it but my mother refuses to take my part. It is a hard thing for her to provide a living allowance to both of us when she has so little to live on herself. And what will Alden do if he does not go back to my uncle? How will he live?"

"Will he attend the university?"

"Alden? No subject could hold his attention long enough for study. He scorns my love of learning."

"What of Dr. Chapman? Now that he has been proven innocent surely he will be reinstated? He can help you to return to the university, can't he?"

"I do not know." I hated to have to admit it to her. "I have not seen the doctor since he was released."

She turned from the shelves with an armful of books frowning. "After all you have done to get him released? He has not seen you?"

"My brother went when he was released yesterday but he did not return with Alden. He went to see Mrs. Larrimer."

Ida bent to place the books in the carton on the floor. When she stood back up her jaw was set. "He is still attached to that lady, then?"

"I do not know." I remembered the last time I had seen Marguerite Larrimer, when she stood with her back to me in that hotel room, telling me her version of the story without ever mentioning William Jones or Ronald Johnson. She had claimed then that she still loved Stephen Chapman.

Frown lines creased Ida's normally smooth brow but before she could speak we heard footsteps and my mother entered, followed by Dean Talbot.

"Emily, see who is here."

I was embarrassed. I had received several notes from the Dean but I had not responded. Now, she was here and I had very little to say for myself.

My mother and Ida excused themselves, leaving us to a private interview, an action which only increased my discomfort.

"I am so sorry, Miss Talbot. After all that you and Mrs. Palmer have done to assist me, I have failed you in the end."

"Emily, I left messages. You should have returned them. You do owe us some consideration. Twice Mrs. Palmer and I have staked our reputations to recommend you. As your reputation is stained, it spreads to us and, more importantly, to the others. What were you doing in that gambling tent? I must demand an explanation."

I tried to explain the plan that had led me to hide and watch through the peephole. It sounded as foolish and ill-judged as I knew it to be by the terrible consequences. She watched me with a frown, only pursing her lips and shaking her head slightly when I forced myself to describe the death of Teddy Hanover.

"I see. Of course your mother told me all of that when she came to me but I wanted to hear it from you. I understand your efforts did expose the truth about the death of Mr. Larrimer, even if that did not become public. In this case, I fear even if a full explanation were publicly known it would not help."

"Despite the fact that Dr. Chapman is released?"

"Even if all the circumstances were known, the notoriety would be seen as far too damaging to the university, especially since we are always attempting to raise funds from our Chicago neighbors. But you must see that expulsion of Dr. Chapman will not reflect on the other men. With time, if he wishes, he will be able to return. But your disgrace will affect the hopes of all the other women. Your failure is a failure for all of us." She held my gaze with an imperious stare until she was satisfied that I understood the gravity of my offense, then she continued, "But I have a plan. Have you heard of Hull House?"

"The settlement house run by Miss Addams?"

"Yes. Mr. Small, the chairman of your department, agreed with Professor Lukas on the necessity for your expulsion. But they do not agree on everything. The settlement house movement is an issue where they are deeply at odds."

"I have heard Mr. Lukas dismiss such efforts as insignificant."

"He derides them, most particularly because women are often the movers behind such efforts. But Mr. Small is a great friend to Jane Addams and Hull House. He disputes the claims of Lukas that they are not worthy of serious consideration. He often visits Hull House to lecture. Like many, he has been converted by Miss Addams."

Many famous people supported the settlement house that Jane Addams had established in a poor immigrant neighborhood on the west side of the city. Its doings were often reported in the newspapers and it had a great popular appeal. Miss Talbot was rubbing her gloved hands together, swinging the reticule that hung from her wrist.

"Miss Addams is a curious personality. Apparently she was inspired by a visit to desperately poor prostitutes in England and on her return she started Hull House on the model of London's Toynbee Hall." The Dean folded her hands together and brought them to her chin, gazing off as if seeing a picture in the air. "Her efforts seem not to be grounded in any firm set of beliefs but rather in a somewhat vague philosophy of the merits of communal living and of learning from the poor." This seemed to puzzle the Dean, but she released her hands and shook her head as if to dispel the image. "But she manages to gather around her active people of firm principles capable of carrying out ambitious plans. They have only just completed a detailed survey of the households in their neighborhood which Mr. Small believes will be a landmark document when it is finally published."

She looked at me sharply. "Miss Addams manages to exist quite outside the boundaries of accepted propriety without offending or being excluded from the best houses and society of the city. Notoriety does not frighten her—she is oblivious to it. Miss Addams has entreated Dr. Chapman, since he is barred from study at the university, to come and join them. In the circumstances, it is the perfect place for you to continue serious work without regard to what has happened."

"Me?"

"I have mentioned you to her and she has assured me you would be welcome to join them. It is a most economical situation and at the same time there are many opportunities to study and work on the type of social problems that interest you. You are ideally suited to thrive there. I have no doubt you will find yourself immersed in activities of great significance. Furthermore, Mr. Small cannot fail to hear of your accomplishments and to regret that you are no longer attached to the university. He has often complained that he is unable to convince several of the women of Hull House to enroll in his department as they are too busy with their own work. I am convinced within a short time he will be anxious to have you back."

She was very happy with this prospect but I slid down on to one of the packing boxes, trying to understand what such an assignment would mean for me.

"I had thought to return to Boston with my mother," I told her. "To teach again."

"Oh, Emily. Now is not the time to retreat. How can you think of it? This is an opportunity to rectify the situation. I know you have the ability to do it." I think it disappointed her that I showed no immediate enthusiasm for the plan. She stood as tall as her small stature would allow and faced me squarely. "But it is your affair—you must decide. Come to me tomorrow morning at Foster Hall if you want to take this up and we will make the arrangements. But now, if you will guide me out of this maze, there is a meeting I must attend at the university."

I attempted to thank her for her efforts on my behalf but she was impatient to be away, so I led her through the corridors and back to the atrium where Roland continued to play. She stopped for a moment.

"If you are disappointed, Emily, and distressed by the unexpected difficulties you have encountered, you must compare yourself to Miss Wells and her people. Surely they have a more difficult road. How can we become discouraged when we see her continue implacably in the face of a very great injustice, compared to which our struggles must seem trivial."

She was right, of course, and, ashamed at how easily I succumbed to discouragement, I promised to visit her the next day. As she was leaving, Dr. Chapman came through the doorway. I felt a surge of relief at the sight of him. He looked a little thinner, with an expression even more serious than usual, but he appeared so much himself as he had always been that I could hardly believe it. In the course of events I had convinced myself I would never see him again. It was a shock and a release to see him suddenly before us like this. I gulped for air around a substantial lump that suddenly clogged my throat.

Meanwhile, Dean Talbot congratulated him on his release and hurried on her way.

"Miss Cabot, I have to thank you for all of your efforts on my behalf." He took my hand in a movement that was more impulsive than any action I had ever seen him make. I flushed.

"I am afraid my efforts were often clumsy. We are all happy they have finally released you. We can only regret the true circumstances of the murder were not revealed publicly."

"It is something I regret nowhere near as much as I would have regretted hanging. Your brother told me of all your efforts and those of Miss Wells, Mr. Barnett and Detective Whitbread. I am eternally grateful."

"It is a great relief to all of us to have it over."

"Your brother also told me how Mr. Hanover died. I am truly sorry to have been the cause of his death."

"No, Doctor. Prendergast caused it all—not you. My own impulsive foolishness contributed but it was Prendergast who pulled the trigger." I saw before my eyes again the barrel of the gun and smelt the acrid smoke from the shot. I flinched at the memory.

Dr. Chapman held my hand more tightly in both of his. "And it has led to your expulsion. I am so very sorry, Emily. I know how much the fellowship means to you. I promise you I will not rest until it is restored." Suddenly he heard the music. "Is that Roland Johnson?"

"Yes. He, too, celebrates his release from the attic where he was hiding."

"I have come to see him."

The doctor had a determined look on his face. He released my hand and I led him to the atrium, where Roland stopped playing as soon as he saw us. He greeted the doctor eagerly and started to apologize for not coming forward with his testimony.

"It has all worked out for the best. But I have something for you," the doctor told him as he held out an envelope. "It is a letter from Mrs. Larrimer. In it she recounts the truth of what happened to your brother."

Roland's eyes lit up as he took the paper and he rushed to Ida and Mr. Barnett at the other side of the room to show it to them.

"So, in the end, he has exonerated his brother," I said. So that was why Dr. Chapman had gone to Marguerite Larrimer on his release from jail. But what else had passed between them? "It is a very good thing."

"It will not bring his brother back to life but at least it will restore his name."

We stood in silence watching as the others rejoiced in the contents of the letter.

The doctor sighed and turned back to me. "We must petition the university authorities to review their decision about your expulsion. You must allow me to do everything in my power to rectify this." He was looking at me with great concern and I understood that he felt the responsibility for my expulsion deeply.

"Oh, no, Doctor," I said as brightly as possible. "Do not trouble yourself. As a matter of fact I do not wish to return to the university. I have other plans, you see. Why Dean Talbot has only just come to tell me I have been successful in my application to join Miss Addams at Hull House. It is something I have long desired."

I lied. I could not let the man believe he had ruined my plans and destroyed my ambitions. I knew very well that what had gone so very wrong in the gambling tent was my responsibility alone. However much I might want to retreat to Boston and my home, it was not to be. My mother and Dean Talbot wanted me to stay. Undoubtedly they were right and, in any case, I owed it to them to make the attempt. They thought I could still fulfill my ambitions at the university and so did the doctor. But my own faith had been deeply shaken. I had seen what a single-minded ambition could do in the figure of Mr. Prendergast. Was my determination to obtain an advanced degree really any different from his to be corporation counsel? I shivered at the thought. In any case, and above all, I would not have the doctor beholden to me. I could not bear it.

"I understand you also go to Hull House, Doctor. Like me, you are unwelcome in the university now?"

He stood before me with his mouth slightly open. I had shocked him. He soon recovered, however, and it seemed as if his shoulders straightened. "Hull House. You are acquainted with Miss Addams? No? She is a most persuasive lady," he told me. "I have, in the past, assisted with some work in a clinic of the neighborhood at her request. When she heard of my release she entreated me to come and join them." He shrugged. "As you know, this is work I have done before and found frustrating but my income is small and the situation is conveniently economical.

It is true I am presently barred from a formal course of study at the university due to the scandal of my arrest."

"But you were released, you are innocent."

"Thank you. But nonetheless, as you know only too well, scandal is scandal and it is unwelcome there. Yet it will really affect me very little. Dr. Jamieson, an elderly man with whom I had been collaborating, cares nothing for reputation and everything for Mr. Pasteur's germ theory. He has assured me he expects— indeed demands—that I continue with the laboratory work. So banishment from lectures will be a relief rather than a burden.

"But you, Miss Cabot . . . after your experiences . . . no one could blame you if you wished to return to the comfort of your mother's home. But if you still contemplate pursuing the studies that brought you here in the first case, Hull House may well be the place for you. It will not be an easy life but it is sure to be a useful one." He reached for my hand and squeezed it. "Nothing would make me happier than to have you join us there."

I saw that, despite his experiences, the doctor stubbornly clung to the plans that had brought him here. He remained convinced that the research that engaged him was of more importance than any other circumstance. Let all the world be wrongheaded in its opinions, yet still he would do what he had decided was right. He would be disappointed, but not surprised, if others were too weak to follow. The road he had chosen was his essence and there was no question of turning back from it. I feared for him and I missed the pressure of his hand when he drew it away.

My mother and the others joined us then to bid him goodbye as the rain outside became even heavier and beat against the roof. With the doctor there before me I felt relief that the suspense of his imprisonment was finally over. I could believe it now. But my own future seemed clouded and uncertain. I would go to Dean Talbot about the position at Hull House but I hardly knew what to expect of that venture.

I stood for a moment in the doorway, watching his retreating figure. Despite the rain that beat down incessantly, there were crews of men hard at work dismantling the surrounding buildings. All over the fairgrounds, exhibits were being packed up and carted away, sculptures rudely levered from their perches and the very materials of the buildings scavenged and plundered.

The dream of the White City would not survive many more days and, as a matter of fact, only a few weeks later, much of what remained went up in flames, just as the late Mayor Carter Harrison had imagined.

AFTERWORD

*F*or Chicago—the quintessential American city in the "heartland"—the 1893 World's Columbian Exposition was a major entrée onto the world's stage. Like an understudy getting her chance to step into the leading role, Chicago threw everything she had into the performance and drew the attention of the world. As with stage scenery, the backdrop and props were ephemeral. Photographs of the time show huge buildings that look oh-so substantial and impressive yet they were designed to be temporary. Like a fairy city, the White City that was the Fair existed for its brief period, then disappeared.

There are many books and some excellent web sites about the Fair. A really entertaining, and popular, recent account is Erik Larson's *The Devil in the White City: Murder, Magic and Madness at the Fair That Changed America*. One of the murders depicted in that book is the very real assassination of Mayor Carter Harrison by Eugene Patrick Prendergast on one of the final days of the Fair. More closely contemporary accounts that describe the mayor's death, and his speech at the Music Hall, may be found in Willis J. Abbot's *Carter Henry Harrison: A Memoir,* and Claudius Osborne Johnson's *Carter Henry Harrison I, Political Leader.*

Prendergast did shoot the mayor and he was hung for it. He did not kill anyone else, however. The characters of William Jones, Charles Larrimer and Teddy Hanover are all fictitious and, as such, only the author can be blamed for their deaths.

Ida B. Wells-Barnett was really present at the Fair and her pamphlet *The Reason Why the Colored American Is Not in the World's Columbian Exposition: The Afro-American's Contribution to Columbian*

Literature was the inspiration for much of the plot of this book. The Larrimers, and the lynching in the fictitious Sherville, Kentucky, are all figments of the author's imagination. But the other lynchings mentioned in the story are paraphrased from the writings of Wells-Barnett, including her autobiography *Crusade for Justice*.

A biography of Wells-Barnett that appeared after this book was finished is *Ida: A Sword Among Lions* by Paula Giddings. This gives a rich telling of Ida's story that goes way beyond the timeline in this novel.

It seems a peculiarly American predicament that the dream of progress represented by the Fair should obscure the very real injustice that was going on at the same time. I find Ida B. Wells to be a particularly admirable and spunky American woman in her blunt and forthright reporting on the true state of affairs. She did go to England to pursue her anti-lynching campaign after the Fair but she returned to Chicago two years later to marry F.L. Barnett. Wise man that he was, he gave her the newspaper as a wedding gift.

Emily Cabot is intended to represent the type of young woman of the time who was able to complete a college degree but then was stymied by the limited number of roles in which she was allowed to put her education to use. Postgraduate research was just beginning to open up to women. At the request of William Rainey Harper—the young president of the new University of Chicago—Alice Freeman Palmer and Marion Talbot recruited women like Emily, with the intention of opening graduate research to them. Talbot's reminiscences, *More Than Lore,* describe the atmosphere they found, and Thomas Goodspeed's *The Story of the University of Chicago, 1890-1925* records the specifics.

The men and women, like Emily, who came to study social problems, eventually created famous schools of sociology and social work. Some of the real women involved are described in Ellen Fitzpatrick's *Endless Crusade: Women Social Scientists and Progressive Reform*. Emily's expulsion from the university is purely a dramatic fiction designed to land her at Hull House and has no basis in fact.

Of the city people, Fitzgibbons is a fabrication, while police detective Henry Whitbread is loosely based on the real detective, Clifton Wooldridge, who published several books of memoirs including *Twenty Years a Detective*. I have attempted to capture some of the tone and attitude of this real man in Whitbread. Coming through as almost larger than life, he does seem a type of man who would have aligned himself with a progressive like Emily Cabot and my intention is to continue their loose partnership in future novels.

There are a number of websites that cover the World's Columbian Exposition. A useful one published in 1996 is at: *http://xroads.virginia.edu/~MA96/WCE/title.html.* The University of Chicago did an interactive site with Chicago Public Schools at *http://ecuip.lib.uchicago.edu/diglib/social/worldsfair_1893/index.html.* Illinois Institute of Technology has a great site at: *http://columbus.gl.iit.edu/.* Finally, in March 2008 the Urban Simulation team at UCLS made available a 3D simulation of the Fair. It allows you to take a virtual stroll through the fairgrounds: *http://www.ust.ucla.edu/ustweb/Projects/columbian_expo.htm.*

READING GROUP DISCUSSION QUESTIONS
FOR *DEATH AT THE FAIR*

1. Why was the World's Columbian Exposition of 1893 such an important event for the city of Chicago?

2. What is the past relationship of Dr. Stephen Chapman and Marguerite Larrimer? Who was to blame for their broken engagement?

3. What does Marguerite Larrimer tell Emily in the hotel before she leaves for Kentucky? Is she lying? What kind of woman is she? What kind of man was her husband?

4. Why did Ida Wells and her fellow authors choose to write and distribute the pamphlet *The Reason Why the Colored American Is Not in the World's Columbian Exposition*? Do you think their efforts were successful?

5. Why do Emily and Clara argue? Do you think this break will end their friendship? If so, why or why not?

6. In the end, what is the responsibility of the city administration and Fitz in the murder of Larrimer? Do they deserve the blame?

7. Does Emily have to take the blame for the death of Teddy?

8. Who needs to take the blame for the death of the mayor?

LaVergne, TN USA
14 March 2011
220132LV00001B/176/P